MY MUM'S COOKBOOK

ROISIN BIBBY

Published by Box Press, Australia

BOX PRESS
P.O. Box 708, Avalon
NSW 2107 AUSTRALIA

PUBLISHED 1993
Reprint 1995

ISBN 0 646 1463 9

Cover photo of Mum by Dad
Photography by Andrew Southam
Design by Cheryl Collins
Props from Wagga Antique Centre
38 Fitzmaurice St, Wagga Wagga

Produced by
Mandarin Offset, Hong Kong

CONTENTS

ACKNOWLEDGEMENTS

Alexandra the Home Economist in the family.
Deborah, my daughter the Editor. Chris and all
the many people who offered ideas on making
this an everlasting cook book.
Nick and Roz for all their computer help.
Fay for hunting down a beautiful fish for our photography.
My husband Reg and son Laurence for all their
encouragement. Helen for babysitting and Adrian
for checking how to spell wildebeest.

Thanks Mum

FOREWORD

You must admit that most recipe books today are very intimidating with untouchable glossy pages. Heaven forbid you should spill anything on the pages!

Well, My Mum's Cook Book is different...cooking is meant to be fun and her book is. An eclectic selection of wonderful family recipes for the dishes that nourished us through childhood, handed down from one generation of good cooks to the next. Not only a collection of tried-and-true recipes, it's also a collection of stories, tips and ideas.

Like everybody else, Mum has opinions on just about everything. Sometimes she keeps them to herself, more often they wind up in her conversations and now in her books. They change even while she speaks.

Assuming many of you would like to write in this book along with her, she's included a blank chapter at the back for you to scribble in, take notes or use as a place to write up some of your Mum's recipes and handy hints.

You'll find no particular order in this book, the recipes covered are many. Mum began this book with her favourite meal of the week - Irish Breakfast on Sundays. So, if you do plan to write in this book, it's unfair to tell you where to begin and where to leave off.

Have fun – we did!

FOR RHONA

A Word From Mum

When we got married I couldn't even boil an egg and I
wished I had spent more time in the kitchen with Mum as I
was growing up. Needless to say, I have spent many hours on
the phone to Mum taking down quick easy recipes. With
carloads of guests about to arrive or a starving husband to feed,
Mum would always have the answer. This continued for
months and very soon Mum began answering the phone
with..."Mum's Cookbook, here to help you". Then we'd go
into fits of laughter about the whole situation. She was always
so good humoured about it. Now talk about history repeating
itself – my daughter was married recently and guess what?
She can't cook!

Believe me, I begged her to spend some time in the kitchen
to see how the now-expert-me could cook. Instead she calls
me daily, usually in a panic for some quick recipe.
And because of her urgency the recipes consist of a handful of
this, or a cup of that, and always a splash of red or white wine
which, by the way will always save the day. It was during one
of these phonecalls that the idea for this book was born.
Why not publish Mum's Cookbook for all the "I can't boil an
egg" people in the world?

Every Mum has a million recipes she has collected over the
years. Many of my Mum's recipes have rarely seen the light of
day. Others have been used so often the pages are now
tattered and smudged with various sauces, mixes and lots of
love. One of her most loved recipes is her Farmhouse Quiche

– the success of that quiche really went to her head. When she took her first quiche out of the oven there it was, all golden brown on top, with little florets of broccoli peeping through the cheesy top, swathed in layers of filo pastry, and there she was with no one at home to share this masterpiece.

She nearly cried.

Well, there are so many stories to relate and you'll find them popping up throughout the book. I hope they will make you laugh as much as they made my family laugh. I have laughed a lot while compiling this cook book and I'm sure you'll find all sorts of little surprises to tickle and tempt you.

Roisin Bibby

CHAPTER ONE

BREAKFAST

Sunday breakfast – this is always a very special time for us (I suppose it's really brunch because it's usually served around 11am). Everyone looks forward to this meal – sort of brings the family together with all the friends. A really happy occasion and the more people the merrier, especially with a few bottles of champagne popping here and there.

The breakfast consists of huge platters of bacon, eggs (did you know if you keep eggs covered while frying they cook beautifully), tomatoes, mushrooms, a few sausages, bananas, potato bread and soda bread. By the way, we always call it an Irish Breakfast because my Mum is Irish and so is potato and soda bread! Oh! We sometimes add smoked salmon and scrambled eggs to the menu. Sheer indulgence.

milkbottles on the doorstep

MUM'S IRISH BREAKFAST

Serves 10

YOU NEED

10 bottles of champers (only kidding, four
will do the trick)
20 rashers bacon
10 thin beef sausages
6 firm tomatoes
5 bananas (you might think bananas strange
but they do add a unique flavour to any
breakfast – just try it)
3 big handfuls of sliced
button mushrooms
24 eggs
lots of buttery toast

METHOD

Grill the bacon and sausages golden brown, then place them
on a platter and cover with foil in a warm oven. Next, toss
thick slices of tomato, banana, button mushrooms under the
grill and let it all sizzle away in the bacon and sausage fat – a
great way to add flavour (these can all be fried if you prefer).
Cook eggs last with a little butter in deep frying pan over a
low heat and cover. Don't forget the toast!

HINT: If toast burns never scrape with a knife.
Instead rub together and the badly burnt parts will
hardly be noticeable.

POTATO BREAD

Serves 4

YOU NEED

4 large peeled potatoes
2 cups self-raising flour
$^1/4$ cup melted butter
$^1/4$ cup milk
pinch of salt and pepper
extra flour for kneading bread

METHOD

Boil potatoes, then mash and add flour, melted butter, milk,
salt and pepper. Mix thoroughly and then turn out onto a
floured board and knead into a smooth dough.
If it's still feeling sticky, keep sprinkling with flour and
continue kneading.
Shape into thick, flat pancakes and cook on a hot fry pan
sprinkled with flour. When golden brown flip over and cook
other side for a couple of minutes (you may need to keep
adding extra flour to the pan).
Cooking time five minutes.

HINT: potato bread can be made and kept for several days.
Just wrap in foil and store in fridge. See soda bread on
following page for instructions on how to eat.

SODA BREAD

Serves 6

YOU NEED

4 cups self-raising flour
2 teaspoons baking soda
1 $^3/_4$ cups sour milk
(if you haven't got it just add white vinegar
to milk and voila!)

METHOD

Mix dry ingredients together in a large bowl. Add sour milk
and mix well. Turn out onto floured board and knead into a
smooth dough. Divide dough into four sections. Cook on a
hot fry pan on top of stove (make sure fry pan is sprinkled
with flour, as in the potato bread recipe on the previous page)
until golden brown on both sides. Cooking time
approximately ten minutes.

HINT: Soda bread can be kept for several days.
Just wrap in foil and store in fridge. But, the best way to eat
soda and potato bread is hot with so much butter
that it's running down your chin.
And remember – it's not a proper Irish Breakfast unless you
have those wonderful breads to enjoy!

POACHED EGGS

You can buy poaching pans but if you haven't got one here's a
simple way to poach an egg.
Before cracking the egg, pop it into very hot water for about 30
seconds. This will stop the white from spreading in the pan
while you're poaching it.
Now break the egg and slip it into a pan full of very hot water.
Forget all those tips such as adding vinegar or making a
whirlpool. In three to three and a half minutes you'll have a
perfectly poached egg.

SCRAMBLED EGGS
WITH SMOKED SALMON
COUNTRY-STYLE

Serves 4

YOU NEED
6 eggs
$1/4$ cup water (most people use milk but
water makes scrambled eggs lighter)
pinch of salt and pepper
1 teaspoon butter
4 slices smoked salmon

METHOD
Beat eggs until frothy and then add the water, salt and pepper.
Heat fry pan with little butter and add egg mixture. When
almost cooked, add chopped smoked salmon. Careful not to
overcook eggs, they should be moist but definitely not runny.

Before we jump into the next recipe have a few sips of that
bubbly to keep you going. All that cooking is hard work.
Well, it's not really. It's fun but the bubbly makes it more fun!

FRENCH OMELETTE

Serves 2

YOU NEED
4 eggs
4 tablespoons water
pinch salt and pepper
2 teaspoons butter

METHOD
Beat eggs slightly, just enough to blend yolks and whites, add
water, salt and pepper. Put butter in hot omelette pan (if you
don't have an omelette pan an ordinary frying pan will do the
trick), when melted pour in mixture and reduce heat slightly.
As the omelette cooks, lift with a spatula letting the uncooked
part run underneath until all is of a creamy consistency.
The omelette should be creamy inside.
Fold and turn onto hot plate. Don't try to make a large
omelette, rather make several smaller ones.
Cooking time three minutes.

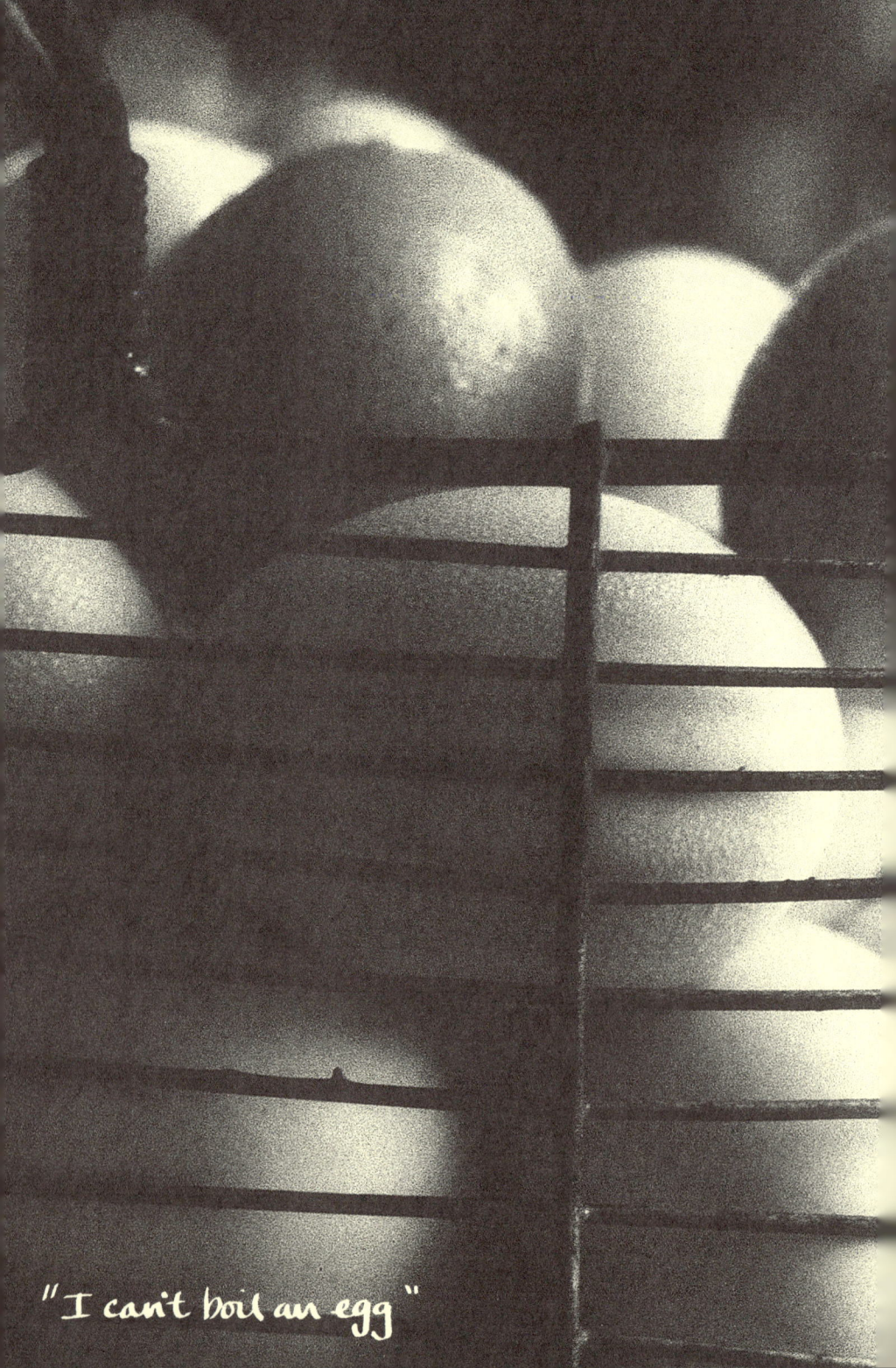

"I can't boil an egg"

VARIATIONS ON
A BASIC OMELETTE

*Before folding, spread with two tablespoons of thickened cream
and fill with the following:*

Bacon: *diced and cooked*

Cheese: *grated and sprinkled on omelette before folding.*

Mushrooms: *sliced and pan fried.*

Parsley and peppers: *cut finely and pan fry before
sprinkling on omelette.*

Ricotta and herbs: *crumble Ricotta, chop fresh herbs and
sprinkle on omelette before folding.*

Spanish: *zuccini, onion, broccoli, green and red peppers,
cheese, tomatoes, mushrooms and a pinch of paprika.
Chop all vegetables finely, cook and sprinkle on
omelette before folding.*

Spinach: *chopped and cooked, sprinkled on omelette
before folding. Cooked in lots of lovely butter.*

Prosciutto: *chopped in cubes and sprinkled on
omelette before folding.*

HINT: *Cheese is wonderful added to all the above recipes
– any cheese*

BOILED EGGS

Now for all those 'can't even boil an egg' people which we talked about earlier on. Select eggs without cracks in the shell and slip them carefully from a tablespoon into a pan of boiling water deep enough to cover the eggs. Reduce heat so that water just simmers. Cook required number of minutes.

Very soft 2 minutes
Soft 3-4 minutes
Firm 5 1/2 - 6 minutes
Hard 9 - 10 minutes

Never fails

EGG AND CHEESE DISH

Serves 2

YOU NEED

2 eggs (separated)

$1/2$ cup cream

2 tablespoons milk

1 $2/3$ cups grated cheddar cheese

2 drops tabasco

pinch paprika

hot brown toast

METHOD

Beat together two egg yolks, and in another bowl beat the
two egg whites together until soft peaks form. Next add the
egg yolks, egg whites, cream and milk together in a small
flame-proof casserole and beat. Place over a low heat and add
cheese. Stir until it's quite thick. Sprinkle in tabasco and
paprika. Take off heat and place in the centre of a warm
platter. Pile pieces of hot buttery toast around it – delicious.
Cooking time three minutes.

FRENCH TOAST

Serves 4 hungry people

YOU NEED

2 eggs

2 tablespoons milk

pinch of salt

3 tablespoons butter

4 thick slices of bread

1 tablespoons cinnamon

1 tablespoon sugar

METHOD

Whisk egg, milk and salt together in a decent size bowl.
Dip bread into mixture. Melt butter in fry pan and fry the
slices until golden brown on both sides. Sprinkle with
cinnamon and sugar. Cooking time two minutes.

EGG IN THE HOLE

Serves 2-4

YOU NEED

4 tablespoons butter

4 slices of thick brown bread

4 eggs

$1/2$ cup grated cheese

1 tomato chopped

METHOD

Melt butter in fry pan. Press out a small round hole from
centre of bread (leave aside, you'll need it later). Place the slice
(with hole) on the buttered fry pan and break egg into the
hole, let fry for 30 seconds. Turn egg 'sunny side up'.
Now, that small round of bread that you left aside – chop it
up and mix with the grated cheese and chopped tomato.
Spoon over egg in the hole and pop it under a hot grill.
Cooking time one minute.

CHAPTER TWO

LUNCH

Every week Mum gives Dad a basket of fresh vegetables
to bring me from their vegie patch. She grows all the
vegetables herself. My Mum is one of those people who
plants something and then just believes it will grow.
She brought all of us up the same way. Secretly though,
she's probably quite puzzled about why the plants grow
so well. She talks to the vegies a lot, the plants thrive
on her conversation and singing. Apparently, there's
nothing a pumpkin likes more than opera!

OCEAN TROUT

Our wonderful fish man always cleans and removes bones and
slits the fish up the middle.
Don't forget to ask to have this done when you buy a whole
fish as it only takes the experts seconds.

Presuming that you have a whole trout ready to stuff: rub the
trout all over, inside and out with vinegar,
then with melted butter. Now for the stuffing:

YOU NEED
1 cup of peeled green prawns
or chopped shrimps
$1/2$ cup crab meat drained (tinned will do)
$1/2$ cup mushrooms sliced
$1/4$ cup breadcrumbs
salt and pepper
1 dash of lemon juice
1 tablespoon chives chopped
$1/4$ cup of white wine or champagne
4 spring onions chopped

METHOD
Preheat oven to 200°f.
Mix all the stuffing ingredients together.
Now stuff the fish and wrap it quite tightly in foil.
Place on baking tray and cook for about 30 minutes at 200°f

HINT: The flesh of the fish should be white, moist and firm,
when cooked through. Allow to cool and serve hot or cold.

P.S. If you prefer another type of whole fish you can still
prepare and cook it the same way as an ocean trout.

ready to bake

BAKED FISH ITALIAN-STYLE

Serves 6

YOU NEED

1 1/2kg firm white fish, cleaned,
boned and sliced
pinch of salt and pepper
1/4 teaspoon chicken stock cube
1 tablespoon flour
1/4 tablespoon paprika
1 cup tomatoes peeled and chopped
1 large onion chopped finely
1/2 green capsicum seeded and chopped
1/2 red capsicum seeded and chopped
1/2 cup spring onions chopped finely
1 cup mushrooms chopped
1/2 cup white wine
1/2 tablespoon melted butter
1 cup breadcrumbs

METHOD

Mix salt, pepper, crumbled chicken stock cube, flour and
paprika together and roll the fish in this seasoning. Put a little
of the peeled tomatoes with the juice in an oven-proof dish
and add the onion and capsicums. Arrange the fish on the
onion and capsicums, cover with the remainder of the
tomatoes and spring onion. Sprinkle with chopped
mushrooms and pour over the wine.
Cover the dish tightly, bake in oven at 450°f for 30 minutes.
Remember to pre-heat grill for the next stage.

WHEN COOKED

Combine the melted butter and breadcrumbs, uncover the fish
dish and spread the buttered breadcrumbs over the top. Put
under grill until nicely browned

CHICKEN, AVOCADO AND CRAB CREPE

Serves 6

YOU NEED

1 tablespoon butter

2 tablespoons flour

$1/4$ cup white wine

1 chicken stock cube

1 cup fresh cream

$1/2$ chicken breast cooked and chopped

$1/2$ cup tinned crab drained and flaked

1 ripe avocado thickly sliced

dash of lemon juice

12 French crepes (see recipe page 186)

$1/4$ cup cheddar cheese grated

METHOD – SAUCE

Melt butter in saucepan, add flour, stir until blended on very
low heat. Then add wine and chicken stock cube.
Stir until it's a smooth creamy mixture.
Lastly add cream, mix well but don't boil!

METHOD – CREPE FILLING

Preheat oven to 300°f.
Mix chicken, crab, avocado and lemon juice together.
Place two good tablespoons of this mixture in the corner of
the crepe, add a tablespoon of the sauce, roll the crepe up.
Repeat this with all the crepes.
Place the crepes in oven-proof dish with rolled side facing
down. Pour remaining sauce over the crepes and sprinkle
cheese over top. Bake at 300°f until heated through.

MUM'S HAMBURGERS

Serves 8

YOU NEED

1 $1/2$ kg best steak minced
$1/2$ packet of seasoned stuffing mix
$1/4$ cup Worcestershire sauce
$1/4$ cup of tomato sauce
1 large onion finely chopped
1 egg
1 beef stock cube crumbled
pinch of salt and pepper

8 onion rings uncooked
8 large bread rolls
1 cup grated cheddar cheese
8 slices tomato
small bowl barbecue sauce

METHOD

Combine first eight ingredients together in a large mixing
bowl. Place on board and divide into eight hamburgers or
patties. Heat a little oil in fry pan until hot. Place four
hamburgers at a time on the pan and fry one side until golden
brown. Turn burgers over and fry other side, then turn heat
down and let cook through. Serve hamburgers on split toasted
bread rolls topped with slices of tomato, grated cheese,
uncooked onion rings and barbecue sauce.
Serve with salad and chips.

P.S. You may grill the hamburgers.
Cooking time seven minutes each side.

CHIP-COATED CHICKEN

Serves 4

YOU NEED

1^1/$_2$ teaspoons curry powder

^{1}/$_4$ teaspoon ginger powder

^{1}/$_4$ cup flour

8 chicken drumsticks

2 eggs (lightly beaten)

2 small packets cheese and
onion crisps crushed

^{1}/$_4$ cup butter

METHOD

Preheat oven to 350°f.

Combine the first three ingredients listed above and roll the chicken drumsticks in this mixture. Dip in egg mixture and roll in the crushed crisps. Melt butter in baking dish, place chicken side by side in baking dish and bake at 350°f.

Cooking time 35 minutes or until tender.

Lovely with rice, and the kids will love it!

LEFT-OVER CHICKEN

Serves 4

YOU NEED
left-over chicken pieces
4 slices ham
asparagus spears tinned and undrained
2 tablespoons flour
2 tablespoons white wine
1 chicken stock cube
2 cups crushed corn flakes

METHOD
Preheat oven to 300°f.
Remove chicken from the bone, cut into small pieces, place
in oven-proof dish and add ham and asparagus, reserving the
liquid. Make a paste with flour and wine, add liquid from
asparagus with stock cube. Pour into dish. Sprinkle corn flakes
over the top. Bake in pre-heated oven for 25 minutes.

QUICHE

They say real men don't eat quiche. Well, it's not true. I've seen real men drool over Mum's quiche and simply beg for the recipe. So for all those drooling real men....

QUICHE BROCCOLI

Serves 8

YOU NEED
10 sheets of filo pastry
$1/4$ cup oil or melted butter
$1/2$ cup grated cheddar cheese
9 florets broccoli boiled for two minutes
6 eggs
2 cups cream
2 level tablespoons cornflour
pinch of salt and pepper
1 chicken stock cube (optional)

METHOD – CASE
Line a large spring baking tin (base lifts out) or large quiche dish with filo pastry, using two sheets at a time which have been brushed with oil or melted butter. Criss-cross pastry until the ten sheets have been used.
Don't forget to brush every two sheets with oil or melted butter. Turn the overlapping sheets back, tucking them in.
Now the case is ready for filling.
See over page for filling.

METHOD – FILLING

Preheat oven to 350°f.

Put the grated cheese into filo case with broccoli. In a big mixing bowl put six eggs, two cups cream, add cornflour, salt and pepper and beat well. Add the crumbled stock cube, beat all together until smooth. Pour this mixture into pastry case, covering the cheese and broccoli. Bake in pre-heated oven for 45 minutes until set and golden brown on top.

HINT: Filo is as light as a feather, contains little butter, no sugar, and it doesn't even need rolling out so it's really easy to work with. The main thing to be aware of is to work quickly so it doesn't dry out. If you want to take it at a more leisurely pace then place the filo under a slightly damp tea towel. This stops it from drying out. The elastic nature of the raw filo dough coupled with its flaky lightness when cooked makes the pastry an ideal wrapper for assorted wonderous fillings.

IMPOSSIBLE QUICHE

Serves 6

If you haven't time to make the famous broccoli quiche with
filo pastry, this one is quick and easy.
Why is it called impossible? Because once made, it looks as if
it was impossible to make. I think it should be called 'magic'
because it separates into layers while cooking.

YOU NEED

4 eggs

1/2 cup plain flour

2 cups milk

1/2 cup melted butter

pinch of salt and pepper

1 cup tinned red salmon separated and
drained

1 onion grated

1/4 cup grated cheese

1/2 packet of savoury biscuits crushed

salt and pepper

METHOD

Preheat oven to 350°f.
Place in a big bowl eggs, flour, milk, melted butter and salt
and pepper. Blend together. Pour this mixture into buttered
oven-proof dish (the mixture should be runny).
Now add red salmon, coarsely grated onion and sprinkle
cheese and crushed biscuits over top. Bake in preheated oven
for 35 minutes until set and golden brown on top.

OTHER QUICHE FILLINGS

There are hundreds of great fillings for quiche.
Here are some of Mum's:

Cheese and Tomato: *slices of tomato, chopped shallots,*
mushroom slices and half cup of cheddar cheese.

Crab and Camembert: *drain and separate a tin of crabmeat.*
Cut Camembert into thin slices and add chopped chives.

Bacon and Onion: *chop cooked bacon into small pieces, grate*
onion, add chopped parsley and half cup of cheddar cheese.

Zucchini and Nutmeg: *two cups of grated zucchini, one cup*
of cheddar cheese grated and half teaspoon of nutmeg.

With all these fillings the eggs, cream, chicken stock and
cornflour are the unchanging ingredients.

MUM'S FRESH VEGIE SALAD

YOU NEED

1 1/2 cups cherry tomatoes

1 cup mushrooms thinly sliced

1 1/2 cups carrots thinly sliced

1 cup broccoli florets

1 cup spring onions sliced

1 cup fresh green beans

YOU NEED – FOR MARINADE

1 clove garlic crushed

1 teaspoon salt

1/2 teaspoon pepper

1 teaspoon chives chopped

1/2 teaspoon dry mustard

1 tablespoon lemon juice

2 tablespoons white wine vinegar

2 tablespoons olive oil

METHOD

Toss broccoli florets and green beans into boiling water for
two minutes. Drain and leave to cool.
Combine all marinade ingredients in a jar.
Shake vigorously and pour over all vegies.

RHONA'S MEAT LOAF

Serves an army

YOU NEED

1 $\frac{1}{2}$ kg best mince
1 large onion chopped finely
2 capsicums seeded and chopped finely
1 cup breadcrumbs
$\frac{1}{4}$ teaspoon salt
$\frac{1}{4}$ teaspoon pepper
$\frac{1}{2}$ teaspoon mustard
1 teaspoon mixed spice
$\frac{1}{2}$ cup tomato juice
2 eggs
$\frac{1}{4}$ cup flour (for board)
4 eggs hard boiled and shelled

METHOD

Preheat oven to 300°f.
Put the first ten ingredients into a large bowl and mix well.
Turn out onto floured board, flatten out and put the hard-boiled eggs along centre of mixture.
Don't forget to shell them (I'm only joking)! Roll the meat mixture around the eggs. Wrap in greased foil, making a package with both ends tucked in securely. Place on baking tray and bake in oven 300°f. Cooking time two hours.

Serve hot or cold.

CHAPTER THREE

THE GOOD SOUP

Is there anything as comforting as a steaming bowl of soup, especially on a cold winter's night, or day for that matter. A bowl of "The Good Soup," Mum used to say, "works wonders". It was quite a normal sight in winter to see a huge pot of soup bubbling away on top of the stove. As far as Mum was concerned it cured every ailment. A warmth to ward off colds and devils.

Minestrone soup, Mum's version of it, has always been a favourite. There's no precise recipe, Mum just loads her minestrone with vegetables to make a hearty and informal meal which leaves one feeling comfortable and warm.

CLEAR STOCK SOUP

YOU NEED

$2^1/_2$ kg bones (poultry, beef, lamb)

14 cups water

1 teaspoon salt

1 potato roughly chopped

1 leek chopped

4 carrots

1 turnip chopped

1 small bunch parsley

2 onions chopped

pinch of salt and pepper

METHOD

Trim and wash bones. Remove the marrow and fat.
Put bones and all other ingredients into a large pot.
Bring to the boil. Let simmer until everything is cooked
through – for four hours approximately. Remove bones and
strain. Let cool and then remove excess fat. This stock can be
refrigerated or frozen for whenever needed.

HINT: Place a piece of bread crust between your teeth and
put on a pair of glasses when peeling and chopping onions.
Believe it or not it does stop you crying.
Yes, I know it sounds ridiculous and you do look
ridiculous but it does work!

LEEK AND POTATO SOUP

Serves 6

YOU NEED

2 tablespoons butter

2 leeks chopped (use only white part)

$1/4$ cup chives or spring onions chopped

2 large potatoes peeled and thinly sliced

6 cups water

2 vegetable stock cubes

$1/4$ teaspoon cayenne pepper

$1/4$ teaspoon pepper

$1/4$ teaspoon salt

1 cup cream

METHOD

Melt butter in a large pot, add leeks and chives or spring
onions. Cook until soft. Add potatoes, water, stock cubes,
peppers and salt, cook until tender. You can serve the soup
just like this, it's delicious or you can... Allow to cool, remove
from pot and blend. Return soup to pot when blended, add
cream and if too thick add extra cream. Keep the soup hot
until ready to serve. Don't boil.

P.S. Don't forget to wash the leeks well and
remove all the grit.

HINT: If ever the soup is too salty add a couple of peeled
raw potatoes, they quickly absorb salt.

VICHYSSOISE

Serves 6

This is a variation of leek and potato soup (page 51).

YOU NEED
1 cup sour cream
1 cup thick cream

METHOD
This is the same recipe as leek and potato soup but when soup
has gone cold, add the sour cream and thick cream.
Blend well and serve chilled.

CROUTONS

Serve with soup

YOU NEED
3 slices of thick bread (crust removed)
2 tablespoons butter

METHOD
Cut slices of bread into tiny cubes. Melt butter in fry pan.
Fry bread until golden brown.

Being Irish, we loved our potato based soups

MINESTRONE

Serves 6

YOU NEED

1 tablespoon oil

2 rashers bacon chopped (remove rind)

2 onions chopped

$1/4$ cabbage chopped

$1/4$ cauliflower chopped

2 carrots chopped

2 leeks chopped

1 small turnip chopped

1 clove garlic crushed

2 cups tinned peeled tomatoes

12 cups water

4 vegetable stock cubes

$1/4$ teaspoon salt

$1/4$ teaspoon pepper

1 cup macaroni

1 cup tinned haricot beans

$1/4$ cup parmesan cheese grated

METHOD

Heat oil in big pot, add bacon and onion and cook over
gentle heat until soft. Add fresh vegetables and garlic,
tomatoes, water, stock cubes and salt and pepper.
Cook 15 minutes, add macaroni, bring soup to boil.
Turn the heat to low and let simmer away gently for half hour
with the lid on pot. Tip in the haricot beans and cook for
another 10 minutes. The soup should be quite thick.
If you prefer it thinner add more water.

Serve in big soup bowls with a liberal sprinkle of parmesan
cheese on top, a crusty loaf and a bottle of red on the side.

Pumpkin Soup

Serves 6

YOU NEED

2 tablespoons butter

1 onion chopped

$1/2$ pumpkin peeled and chopped

2 carrots chopped

2 sticks of celery chopped

$1/2$ teaspoon curry powder

$1/4$ teaspoon salt, $1/4$ teaspoon pepper and

$1/4$ teaspoon nutmeg – mix

seasonings together

6 cups water

2 chicken stock cubes

1 cup cream

$1/4$ cup chives chopped

METHOD

Melt butter in large pot, add onion, pumpkin, carrots, celery and curry powder. Cook for 5 minutes. Add seasonings, six cups of water and stock cubes. Bring to boil and cook gently for 20 minutes or until vegetables are tender. Allow to cool. Remove from pot and blend. If you haven't a blender then rub through a sieve. return to pot and add cream.

Keep the soup hot.

Don't boil.

Serve with a dollop of cream and a few
chopped chives on top.

HINT: This is a great soup to make in bulk.
Simply keep it in the fridge or freezer and when friends pop
around you have a meal in itself ready.

Broccoli And Pinenut Soup

Serves 6

YOU NEED

2 tablespoons butter

1 onion chopped finely

2 vegetable stock cubes

3 handfuls broccoli florets

1 cup white wine

$1/4$ teaspoon salt

$1/4$ teaspoon pepper

1 cup sour cream

3 tablespoons pinenuts

6 cups of water

METHOD

Melt butter in large pot and add onion and cook until soft.
Add remainder of ingredients, except cream and pinenuts.
Bring to boil and cook gently for 15 minutes.
Allow to cool, remove from pot and blend. Return to pot and
add sour cream. Keep hot. Don't boil.

Serve with a dollop of sour cream and pinenuts
sprinkled on top.

IRISH BROTH

Serves 6

YOU NEED

1 marrow bone

6 cups water

1 cup green lentils (no need to soak)

$1/4$ teaspoon salt

$1/4$ teaspoon pepper

2 carrots chopped roughly

2 celery sticks chopped roughly

2 onions chopped

1 turnip chopped

1 parsnip chopped

$1/4$ bunch of parsley chopped

METHOD

Place marrow bone, water and lentils in a big pot with salt and
pepper. Boil for half an hour until lentils are soft. Add the
remaining ingredients and cook gently for one hour.
Serve with thick slices of crusty bread.

FRENCH ONION SOUP

Serves 4

YOU NEED

1 tablespoon olive oil

4 large onions sliced thinly

1 tablespoon butter

1 teaspoon brown sugar

$1/4$ teaspoon salt

$1/4$ teaspoon pepper

$1/4$ cup Sherry

5 cups boiling water combined with 2
vegetable stock cubes

1 cup parmesan cheese grated

1 large baguette (French loaf)

METHOD

Preheat oven to 350°f.

Place oil in fry pan, add onions and fry until soft (but not brown). Add butter, sugar, salt, pepper and Sherry. Put mixture into deep casserole, add water and cover with lid. Cook in oven at 350°f for 30 minutes. When soup is almost ready prepare four thick slices of baguette, liberally sprinkled with parmesan. Pop under hot grill for a few seconds.

Serve soup in deep bowls, top each one with cheesy bread.

GREEN GARDEN SOUP

Serves 6

YOU NEED

2 tablespoons butter
2 leeks washed and sliced
(use only white part of leek)
1 potato peeled and chopped
2 zucchinis chopped
1 cup spinach chopped
$1/4$ cup lemon juice
1 cup peas (fresh or frozen will do the trick)
2 cups lettuce shredded
4 celery stalks chopped
$1/4$ cup parsley
2 tablespoons mint leaves chopped
pinch salt and pepper
10 cups water
2 vegetable stock cubes

METHOD

Melt butter in large saucepan. Add leeks, potato, zucchinis,
spinach and lemon juice. Cook gently for ten minutes.
Next add peas, lettuce, celery, parsley, mint, salt and pepper.
Add ten cups of water and finally the vegetable stock cubes.
Cook for 20 minutes. Allow to cool and then blend well.

This soup is best served chilled.

Don't throw the stalks out - they're great added to mushroom soup.

CHAPTER FOUR

HORS D'OEUVRES

Well, it had to happen. Mum and Dad bought a little restaurant. It was really cute but needed 'Tender Loving Care' and a little time to build up the clientele. The restaurant was opened evenings only. At the start it was quite nerve-wracking and it wasn't unusual around about six o clock in the evening to find Mum kneeling behind the cocktail bar, a glass of sherry in one hand with her eyes cast up towards the heavens. The first time I saw her do this I asked Mum, what on earth are you doing . "I'm just asking God to get that telephone ringing. We've only got five bookings tonight". As she got off her knees the phone started ringing and bookings would come in fast and furious. By eight o'clock the restaurant was packed. This happened time after time and I think she really had a direct link with 'What's His Name'.

Sometimes it was a very long night and occasionally it could be difficult to get the last few diners to go home. She had one little trick to move them without appearing rude and that was to play a tape of 'The Flight of the Bumble Bee' by Rimsky Korsakov very loudly. That worked – late night diners almost tripped over themselves to get out of there and I don't blame them.

Mum and Dad's restaurant became the in-place to go
and many fun times were had there.

The food was so good, a customer made Dad an offer
to buy the place so they sold it and a lot of people were
sad to see them go. Never mind, they made heaps of
friends and you can never have too many of those.

Now, back to recipes – as well as Mum's family recipes
I've included some favourite hors d'oeuvres from
the little restaurant, enjoy.

OYSTERS KILPATRICK

Serves 6

YOU NEED

18 opened oysters (in the shell, of course!)
9 rashers bacon chopped (without the rind)
Worcestershire sauce

METHOD

Chop bacon finely. Put a few pieces on each oyster.
Sprinkle Worcestershire sauce liberally over bacon and oysters.
Place under hot grill until bacon is crispy.
Be careful not to overcook.
Serve hot, and pop open a bottle of your
favourite champagne.

MOCK CRAYFISH

Serves 6

YOU NEED

1 tablespoon butter

1 onion finely chopped

6 spring onions chopped finely

4 large filets of firm white boneless fish

$1/4$ cup dill chopped

pinch salt and pepper

3 avocados, firm but ripe

YOU NEED – SAUCE

1 cup tomato sauce

1 cup mayonnaise

$1/2$ teaspoon tabasco

1 teaspoon Worcestershire sauce

$1/2$ cup lemon juice

1 dash sherry

pinch salt and pepper

Blend all sauce ingredients together

METHOD – FISH

Melt butter in fry pan, toss in the onion and spring onion
and cook until soft. Add fish and cook very gently in
butter and seasoning for ten minutes.
The fish should look firm and white. Remove the fish, when
the fish is cold, gently flake (separate). Now you have all that
lovely cold fish, just pour the sauce over it. Cut the avocados
in half, lengthwise, and sprinkle a little lemon juice over them
to keep them from going brown.
Fill each half with the fish and sauce mixture, add dill
for decoration and that is Mock Crayfish.
Keep refrigerated until ready to serve.

SMOKED SALMON AND CAVIAR

Serves 4

YOU NEED

1 butter lettuce (if you're not sure ask your green grocer)
8 slices smoked salmon

YOU NEED – FILLING

1 cup cream cheese
$1/4$ tablespoon lemon juice
$1/2$ cup caviar
pinch salt and black pepper
1 handful chives chopped

METHOD

Mix the filling ingredients together and place a spoonful of the
filling on each slice of salmon. Then roll up in the salmon.
Serve on a leaf of butter lettuce and add
cherry tomatoes for colour.

P.S. This is an easy hors d'oeuvres and especially good
if you're in a hurry.

DEEP FRIED CAMEMBERT
AND CRANBERRY SAUCE

Serves 6

YOU NEED

12 wedges of Camembert

2 eggs beaten

1 cup breadcrumbs dry

1 tablespoon fresh parsley chopped

pinch salt and pepper

2 cups oil

METHOD

Dip wedges of Camembert in beaten egg and then in seasoned
breadcrumbs mixed with salt, pepper and parsley. Deep fry in
hot oil until golden brown which takes about a minute.
If you have time it's better to refrigerate the crumbed wedges
before deep frying for about half an hour. Serve the
Camembert wedges with a drizzle of cranberry sauce.

CRANBERRY SAUCE

YOU NEED

2 cups tinned cranberries

3 tablespoons orange juice

2 tablespoons sherry

1/4 cup water

METHOD

Place all the ingredients in saucepan and bring to boil.
Cook gently for ten minutes. Strain.

MUSHROOMS FARCI
WITH PARMA HAM

Serves 4

YOU NEED

8 large mushrooms wiped with
stalk removed
3 tablespoons butter
1 onion chopped finely
2 slices parma ham chopped
1 egg beaten
1/4 cup cheddar cheese grated
1 tablespoon chives

METHOD

Wipe mushrooms really well and remove stalks. Melt butter in
fry pan, add onion and fry until soft. Remove from heat and
stir in the beaten egg, chopped ham, cheese and chives.
Place mushrooms (hollow side facing up) in an oven-proof
dish. Pile the filling into each mushroom and bake in oven for
15 minutes. If you would like the mushrooms nice and crisp
on top, then pop them under the grill for a few minutes.

P.S. Mum says it is not necessary to wash the mushrooms or
peel them. Just wipe them really well. They keep their flavour
better. And don't throw the stalks out they're great
added to mushroom soup.

CRAB AVOCADO

Serves 4

YOU NEED
1 cup tinned crab (drained)
1 avocado (ripe)
salt and pepper to taste
$^1/4$ cup lemon juice
2 tablespoons mayonnaise

METHOD
Mix together and spoon onto centre of your favourite plate.
Chill and serve with crisp green salad.

PROSCIUTTO AND MELON WRAP AROUNDS

Serves 6

YOU NEED

1 rock melon peeled and cut in small wedges

12 slices prosciutto thinly sliced

MARINADE – YOU NEED

2 tablespoons honey

$1/4$ teaspoon black pepper

2 tablespoons white wine

METHOD

Combine marinade ingredients, wrap prosciutto around melon. Drizzle marinade over melon and prosciutto.

HINT: Never say to your guest "I made this dish especially for you". If they hate it they'll end up feeding it to the cat, stuffing it in their pockets or into the floral arrangements!!!

CRAB, CHICKEN AND
AVOCADO BAKES

Serves 6-8

YOU NEED

8 tablespoons butter

1 onion chopped finely

$1/2$ teaspoon fresh rosemary

$1/2$ teaspoon paprika

2 chicken stock cubes crumbled

1 tablespoon flour

$1/2$ cup white wine

1 cup water

1 cup chicken chopped

1 avocado peeled and chopped

1 cup tinned crab drained

1 tablespoon fresh dill

1 cup sour cream

1 cup breadcrumbs

METHOD

Preheat oven to 300°f.
Use four tablespoons butter and melt in fry pan. Add chopped
onion and cook until soft. Now add the rosemary, paprika and
crumbled stock cubes. Stir well and add the flour and gently
pour in the wine. Stir until blended and then add the water
and stir again. By this time you should have a nice creamy
sauce. Now add the chicken, avocado and crab, plus the dill.
Lastly, pour in the sour cream. Heat well but don't boil.
Spoon the mixture into individual oven-proof dishes, six or
maybe eight. Mix the breadcrumbs with remaining butter and
spread over the crab mixture. Now they're ready to bake.
Bake for 15 minutes in oven of 300°f.
Then pop under grill until golden brown

CALAMARI

Serves 4

YOU NEED
2 cups oil
20 rings calamari
4 tablespoons plain flour
$^1/_2$ cup beer
extra flour in which to roll calamari

METHOD
Heat the oil until hot in deep fry pan. Roll the calamari in
flour then make a light batter with the four tablespoons of
flour and half a cup of beer. The batter mixture should be
thin. Dip each calamari ring into the batter. Place a few rings
at a time into the very hot oil. The calamari will become
golden very quickly. It only takes seconds to cook
(If you overcook calamari it becomes tough).
Remove from oil and drain on newspaper.
Lovely served with tartare sauce (see recipe page 103)
or a tangy sauce.

Skewered Bananas With Bacon

Serves 6-8

YOU NEED

4 bananas

8 rashers bacon (without rind)

2 tablespoons oil

8 skewers

METHOD

Preheat the grill.

Peel and cut bananas into four pieces. Cut bacon in two pieces, wrapping each piece of bacon around a piece of banana. Thread three pieces on each skewer (securing bacon at the same time) and brush with a little oil.

Cook under moderate grill until bacon is crispy.

Serve with salad. Cooking time 6-8 minutes.

ASPARAGUS

*Some people make such a fuss about cooking asparagus. Mum's
is always lovely. She just cuts the white stalk off then scrapes
the spear from the tip downwards to give it an extra clean.
Then she pops them into salted boiling water for ten minutes or
until tender. Drain water, add squeezed lemon
and butter. Delicious!*

HINTS

You'll notice that Mum has used stock cubes in most of her savoury dishes – she even uses a touch of chicken stock in one of her fish recipes when she was stuck for the real thing. The important thing is flavour.

Before you pop that roast beef or chicken in the oven crumble a stock cube and rub it into the meat.

Add a stock cube to the sediment in the roasting pan to make your gravy.

How many times have you tried a recipe to find it has something missing?
Well, that's when you toss in a stock cube – they bring out the flavour. You can get chicken, beef, mushroom, vegetable and bacon stock cubes in most supermarkets.
So buy a selection next time you're shopping and make the most of them.

CHAPTER FIVE

DINNER

Mum makes the best chips in the whole world and I'll
tell you why. My Dad has chips every night, even
before I was born Mum made chips for Dad. We could
be having the most sumptuous meal and guess what?
Out comes the chip pan! Mum says that when Dad dies
his epitaph will probably read "Goodbye Mr Chips".

Mum has already planned her own wake. She wants
smoked salmon served with chilled champagne and
Mozart filling the air. She says, "If you don't like
Mozart then don't bother coming to my wake."
After all that... you'll find the famous chip recipe
in this chapter.

CHIPS

Serves 2

YOU NEED

3 large potatoes, peeled and chopped
in long thick slices
1 bottle oil
1 teaspoon salt

METHOD

Roll chips dry in towel to rid them of excess water. Heat oil
in a deep pan. Drop one chip in to test the oil – when the
chip rises to the surface the oil is ready. Drop the chips gently
into the hot oil and cook until golden brown and crispy.
Remove from oil and drain on newspaper.
Be careful not to burn yourself. Sprinkle with a little salt
which brings out the flavour.

HINT: A chip pan with a frying basket does
make cooking chips a lot easier and you're less likely to get
splashed with hot oil.

The humble spud does come in handy... If your windscreen
wiper is out of order during rainy weather, cut a raw potato in
half and wipe it over the windscreen. The rain will run
straight down the glass and you will have perfect vision.
Who needs wipers??

Mr Chips, thats Dad's nickname

MONEY BAGS STEAK

Serves 6

Mum called this Money Bags Steak because she always used
fillet and it's quite expensive. So it's a real treat.
I love the sauce.

YOU NEED

6 thick slices fillet steak

$1/2$ cup onion chopped finely

2 cups mushrooms chopped finely

1 tablespoon dry mustard

1 cup tomato sauce

$1/2$ cup red wine

1 cup Worcestershire sauce

2 tablespoons butter

2 tablespoons white vinegar

$1/2$ clove garlic crushed

2 dashes tabasco (optional)

decent pinch of salt and pepper

METHOD

In large fry pan, brown the steak on both side sealing in juices.
Set aside the steaks. In same fry pan brown onion and
mushrooms in the butter and add the rest of the ingredients.
Cook for a further five minutes. Add the steaks to the
mixture, heat well and cook to rare–medium.
Wonderful served with French fries or rice.

HINT: The steaks will be a little rare so if you prefer them
well done then cook them for a little longer

Chicken Fillets With Prosciutto And Camembert

Serves 4

YOU NEED

4 small chicken fillets

8 slices of Camembert cheese

pinch salt and pepper

1 teaspoon rosemary

8 thin slices prosciutto

2 tablespoons butter

METHOD

Cut a shallow slit in the chicken fillets and stuff each fillet with two slices of Camembert cheese. Season with salt, pepper and rosemary. Wrap a slice of prosciutto around each chicken fillet and secure with tooth pick. Pan fry gently in butter for ten minutes each side of fillet until cooked through. Remove chicken fillets from pan and save the juices for the sauce. Keep them warm. Don't forget to remove tooth picks.

SAUCE – YOU NEED

4 spring onions finely chopped

$^1/4$ cup white wine

dash of brandy

$^1/4$ cup cream

METHOD

Place the fry pan over a low heat on top of stove and add spring onions to the juices. Fry gently for three minutes. Add white wine and brandy, simmer, add cream and heat through. Serve chicken fillets on a bed of sauce.

GRANDMA LA LA'S
ROAST CHICKEN

Serves 6

YOU NEED

1 large roasting chicken
$^1/_4$ teaspoon salt, $^1/_4$ teaspoon pepper,
1 teaspoon paprika, 1 tablespoon powdered
ginger (mix all these seasoning
ingredients together)
2 tablespoons oil
1 cup white wine or champagne
2 chicken stock cubes crumbled

METHOD

Preheat oven to 400°f.
Rinse chicken in cold water and dry, rub the seasonings into
the skin of the bird. Place it in a roasting dish, breast side up.
Drizzle the oil over top of chicken, pour half cup of wine into
the roasting dish. Roast in oven of 400°f for 15 minutes, turn
chicken over on other side and roast for another ten minutes.
Reduce the heat to 380°f, continue roasting another half hour,
spooning the liquid over the chicken occasionally and adding
the remainder of the wine.
Pierce the chicken on breast with a fork – if the juices
running out are clear then the chicken is cooked.
Place the chicken on platter and keep warm in oven until
serving. Add stock cubes to pan juices and simmer gently for
eight minutes – this will give you a lovely sauce.

GRILLED MARINATED
BABY CHICKENS

Serves 4

YOU NEED
4 baby chickens cut in half

MARINADE – YOU NEED
Combine followings ingredients:

$1/2$ cup white vinegar

2 tablespoons soya sauce

2 tablespoons crushed garlic

1 tablespoon ginger

1 tablespoon Worcestershire sauce

1 $1/2$ tablespoons soft brown sugar

1 cup oil

1 tablespoon curry powder

1 tablespoon basil

1 large onion finely chopped

1 tablespoon paprika

METHOD
Place chickens in roasting pan, pour the marinade over chickens. Cover and refrigerate all day if possible or for an hour or so before grilling. Remove chicken from refrigerator and place the roasting pan with chicken and marinade under a hot grill. Grill skin side of chickens and then turn and grill other side, spooning the marinade over the chickens frequently. The skin of the chicken should be golden brown and crispy. Cooking time about 20 minutes.
Serve with potato puffs (see recipe on page 133)
and a cool green salad.

ANN SPANN'S BURGUNDY PORK CHOPS

Serves 4

YOU NEED

8 pork loin chops
$1/4$ teaspoon salt
$1/4$ teaspoon pepper
$1/4$ cup plain flour
2 tablespoons oil
2 tablespoons butter
1 teaspoon cornflour
2 tablespoons French mustard
1 tablespoon soft brown sugar
1 cup Burgundy wine
1 cup pineapple pieces drained

METHOD

Preheat oven to 370°f.
Roll chops in flour salt and pepper. Heat oil in fry pan and
brown chops on both sides. In a saucepan melt butter.
Add cornflour and stir in blended mustard and brown sugar.
Add wine and pineapple and bring to boil. Arrange chops in
oven-proof dish. Pour the sauce over the chops and cover
with tinfoil. Bake in moderate oven at 370°f until chops are
tender for approximately 45 minutes.
Remove tinfoil for last ten minutes of baking.

BEEF WELLINGTON

Serves 6

YOU NEED

1 $^1/_2$ whole beef fillet (fat removed)

1 tablespoon vinegar

2 tablespoons butter

$^1/_4$ cup plain flour

$^1/_4$ teaspoon brown sugar

1 teaspoon dry mustard

pinch salt and pepper

$^1/_4$ cup red wine

3 slices chicken pate (optional)

1 tablespoon tomato puree

2 tablespoons red wine

2 tablespoons brandy

2 cups mushrooms, fresh and chopped

1-2 ready rolled puff pastry sheets

1 egg yolk lightly beaten

METHOD

Preheat oven to 450°f.

Brush the beef fillet with vinegar.

Melt butter in large fry pan (an electric fry pan can be used)
and quickly brown the meat all over. Remove fillet from pan.

In a bowl, combine the flour, sugar, mustard, salt and pepper.

Roll the meat in the flour mixture and place it in a large
baking dish with quarter a cup of red wine.

Roast in a moderately hot oven at 450°f for ten minutes.

Take the meat out of the oven to cool.

Next combine the chicken pate, tomato puree, two
tablespoons red wine, two tablespoons brandy and the
mushrooms in a big bowl.

For how to assemble beef wellington see over page.

83

How To Assemble
Beef Wellington

Place the beef fillet in the centre of 1-2 sheets of ready rolled puff pastry (the number depends on the size of the fillet). Spread the mushroom and pate mixture over the top of the fillet. Wrap the beef fillet up in the pastry, like a neat and tight parcel. Brush pastry parcel with the lightly beaten egg yolk. Place the parcel with folded side down on a lightly oiled baking dish and bake in a moderate oven at 370°f for approximately 20 minutes or until pastry is golden brown. Remove beef parcel from baking dish and keep the dripping for the sauce. Place beef parcel in a warm oven on oven proof dish till ready to serve.

HINT: To decorate Beef Wellington – before placing in oven – cut strips of pastry and wrap around parcel at even intervals. Brush with beaten egg yolk.

Brandy sauce for Beef Wellington next page.

Brandy Sauce
For Beef Wellington

YOU NEED

2 tablespoons red wine

2 tablespoons brandy

1 beef stock cube

2 tablespoons plain flour

1 cup hot water

METHOD

Place the baking dish over a moderately high heat on top of
the stove. Be careful not to burn it.

Add the red wine, brandy, crumbled stock cube, flour and
water. Gently boil for five to ten minutes until sauce has
slightly thickened.

Serve Beef Wellington in thick slices with your
brandy sauce – heaven!

P.S. If gravy is too thin add a little blended flour and water.

P.P.S. If gravy is lumpy then strain it.

ROAST BEEF AND YORKSHIRE PUDDING

Serves 8

YOU NEED
2 kg roast beef

$^1/_4$ cup flour, 1 beef stock cube, $^1/_4$ teaspoon
salt, $^1/_4$ teaspoon pepper (mix these
seasonings together)

$^1/_4$ cup oil

1 carrot roughly chopped

1 onion roughly chopped

METHOD
Preheat oven to 400°f.

Roll beef in seasoning.

Place it in roasting dish with the fatty side up.

Pour oil over meat and place in oven at 400°f to brown and
seal in the juices for about ten minutes.

Turn the meat over to brown all sides.

Reduce the oven heat to 300°f and continue roasting with the
carrot and onion added until it is done to your taste: rare,
medium or well-done. Roasting times: 35 minutes per kg –
underdone, 45 minutes per kg – well done.

For gravy see next page.

YOU NEED – GRAVY

2 tablespoons flour

1 beef stock cube

$^1/_2$ cup water

1 cup red wine

METHOD

Remove beef from roasting dish and keep warm.
Place dish over moderately hot heat on top of stove.
Add flour and cook until light brown. Add red wine and stock
cube and gently simmer. If gravy is too thick add the water.
Strain and keep hot.

HINT: If you have burning fat in the oven it can be quite
frightening but just sprinkle salt over flames and
they'll go out instantly.

Yorkshire Pudding over page.

YORKSHIRE PUDDING

This mixture is best if allowed to stand for a couple of hours.
Perhaps prepare the mixture just before embarking on
the roasting of the beef.

YOU NEED

1 $^1/_2$ cups plain flour

$^1/_4$ teaspoon salt

$^1/_4$ teaspoon pepper

2 eggs

1 cup milk

3 tablespoons fat from roasting dish

METHOD

Preheat the oven to 450°f.

Place the flour, salt and pepper in a mixing bowl and make a
well in the centre. Add one egg and mix and then add the
other egg and mix gently. Add milk, a little at a time, beating
constantly – all the flour should now be combined with eggs
and milk. The mixture should be like thick cream.

Let mixture stand as long as possible.

Twenty minutes before you are ready to serve the roast beef,
place three tablespoons of very hot roasting fat in oven-proof
dish. Pour the batter in and bake in a very hot oven at 450°f
for 15 minutes until puffed up and golden brown.

No peeping in the oven until the 15 minutes are up.

Serve straight from oven with the Roast Beef.

HINT: Roast Beef and Yorkshire Pudding is lovely served
with crisp roast potatoes, carrots and good
old-fashioned beans.

BAY'S CHICKEN

Serves 6

YOU NEED
4 tablespoons butter
2 boneless chicken breasts, cooked
and chopped
1 onion finely chopped
1 cup mushrooms sliced
$1/2$ green capsicum, seeded and
finely chopped
$1/2$ red capsicum, seeded and finely chopped
4 tablespoons plain flour, pinch salt and
pepper, $1/2$ teaspoon paprika combined
1 tablespoon lemon juice
3 chicken stock cubes, 3 cups boiling water
mixed together
$1/2$ cup dry sherry
1 cup cream
2 egg yolks

METHOD
Melt butter in large pan, fry chicken until tender. Leave aside,
fry onion until soft, add mushrooms and capsicums. Stir in
flour mixture and lemon juice. Add chicken stock, cook
gently for ten minutes. Add cooked chicken, sherry and lastly
the cream and egg yolks. Heat through.
In the meantime have a little glass of sherry yourself and
prepare rice and salad for a perfect accompaniment.

ROAST LEG OF LAMB
WITH MINT SAUCE

Serves 8

YOU NEED
large leg of lamb
1 tablespoon flour, $^1/_4$ teaspoon salt,
$^1/_4$ teaspoon pepper, 1 teaspoon rosemary,
1 teaspoon basil (mix all these seasoning
ingredients together)
1 clove garlic
$^1/_2$ cup white wine

METHOD
Preheat oven to 300°f.
Rub the seasoning over the leg of lamb and push the clove of
garlic under the skin of the lamb.
Place the lamb in roasting dish skin side down add wine and
cook for approximately two hours in a slow oven. Pierce with
fork and if juices are clear the lamb is cooked.

For Mint Sauce see next page – a must with Roast Lamb.

MINT SAUCE

YOU NEED

2 tablespoons boiling water

$^1/_2$ cup mint chopped finely

1 tablespoon castor sugar

$^1/_2$ cup white vinegar

METHOD

Add boiling water to mint and sugar, then add vinegar.
Allow to stand for ten minutes or so before serving.

Serve with roast potatoes, green beans and
butternut pumpkin.

HINT: This sauce will keep indefinitely if kept in an airtight
container in the fridge.

BARBECUED SPARE RIBS

Serves 6

YOU NEED
2 kg of beef or pork spare ribs

Mix the following together:
5 tablespoons honey
2 tablespoons brown sugar
3 tablespoons soya sauce
1 clove garlic crushed
$^1/_4$ cup sherry
3 tablespoons vinegar

You might want more sauce for the ribs if so, just double the above ingredients.

METHOD
Get the butcher to cut the spare ribs into the portions you require. Put the ribs in a big pot and cover with boiling water. Cook for ten minutes and then throw the water away. Place the ribs in grilling pan or dish and pour half the sauce over them. Grill until crisp on all sides. Brush remainder of sauce over the ribs and cook for a little longer.

HINT: If you prefer they can be barbecued.

IRISH STEW
WITH DUMPLINGS

Serves 6

Mum used to say Irish Stew sticks to your bones. Well, it must as it's so nourishing and so cheap to make. It should be made with neck of lamb, but Mum always uses the trimmed small lamb loin chops so here it is...

YOU NEED
12 lamb loin chops trimmed

6 tablespoons butter

1 large onion chopped roughly

2 large carrots chopped roughly

6 large potatoes peeled and cut in quarters

$1/4$ teaspoon salt

$1/4$ teaspoon pepper

3 cups boiling water

2 beef stock cubes

METHOD
In large pot brown the chops and onion in the butter. Cover this with boiling water and gently cook for half an hour. Add carrots, beef stock cubes, potatoes, salt and pepper, and gently cook until the potatoes break up and the stew becomes thick.

If the water boils off simply continue to add more water to keep the stew moist.

Dumplings over page.

DUMPLINGS
FOR IRISH STEW

YOU NEED

2 cups self-raising flour

2 teaspoons baking powder

1 cup milk

(if you're out of milk water will do the trick)

salt and pepper

METHOD

Mix the flour, baking powder, salt and pepper together. Add
the milk gradually and mix well. Mixture should not be
runny. When the stew is almost ready, drop tablespoons of
dumpling mixture into the stew. Let the dumplings gently
cook. Make sure the lid is kept tightly on the pot. When the
dumplings are ready they will be firm to touch.

My Mum always serves Irish stew and dumplings with thick
slices of brown bread.
She says "It brings me back to base roots"

CHAPTER SIX

SAUCES AND DRESSINGS

Until you try,
you don't know
what you cannot do.

White Sauce

1 tablespoon butter
2 tablespoons plain flour
1 cup milk
pinch of salt and pepper
1 chicken stock cube (optional)
$^1/_4$ cup white wine (optional)

Melt butter in saucepan over low heat. Add flour gradually
and stir well until blended. Gradually add milk, salt and
pepper, stirring continuously. Add crumbled stock cube and
white wine, and stir until thickened.

Brown Sauce

Use the same method as for white sauce but cook the butter
and flour until it's golden in colour. Add a beef stock cube
instead of a chicken cube.

P.S. If there are any lumps in the sauce whisk vigorously
or strain.

*The basic white sauce (above) may have the following added to
accompany different dishes.*

Mustard Sauce

1 tablespoon German grain mustard
1 tablespoon honey
1 dollop of cream
Add to basic white sauce.
And serve with steaks.

the basics

HORSERADISH SAUCE

Add two tablespoons of prepared horseradish sauce to basic
white sauce. Whisk and stir in a dollop of sour cream.
Serve with most red meat.

PARSLEY SAUCE

Add quarter cup of parsley, chopped finely, to white sauce.
Serve with fish.

CURRY SAUCE

$1/2$ teaspoon curry powder

$1/4$ teaspoon ginger

$1/4$ teaspoon paprika

1 tablespoon chutney

Add to basic white sauce and cook through. Wonderful served
with hot, hard boiled eggs. Cut lengthwise.

CHEESE SAUCE

YOU NEED

1 cup grated cheese

$1/4$ teaspoon French mustard

METHOD

Add to basic white sauce mixture. The mustard is optional but
it does bring out the flavour.
Serve with pastas, fish and most savoury dishes.

MUSHROOM SAUCE

Add half cup thinly sliced mushrooms to basic white sauce.
The mushrooms will soften in the hot liquid.
Serve with any savoury dish.

*The basic brown sauce (see page 96) may have the following
ingredients added to it to accompany different dishes.*

PEPPER SAUCE I

YOU NEED
^{1}/2 teaspoon crushed black pepper
^{1}/4 cup brandy
1 dollop of cream
1 teaspoon brown sugar

METHOD
Mix together. Add to basic brown sauce (see page 96).
Serve with steaks.

PEPPER SAUCE II

YOU NEED
1 teaspoon crushed peppercorn
splash brandy
dollop of cream

Pan fry thick slices of beef fillet in two tablespoons of butter.
Cook to required taste. Remove beef from pan and keep
warm. Add to the sediment left in pan one teaspoon of
crushed peppercorn, a splash of brandy. Cook for 30 seconds,
add a dollop of cream and quickly heat through.
Also lovely served with veal.

Napoli Sauce

YOU NEED

4 tablespoons butter

$1/2$ cup bacon chopped finely
(without the rind)

$1/4$ cup onion chopped finely

$1/4$ cup celery chopped finely

$1/2$ cup tinned tomatoes drained and chopped

1 clove garlic crushed

METHOD

Cook all the ingredients in butter until browned.
Add to brown sauce (page 96).
Serve with pasta or polenta (see polenta recipe on page 113).

Orange Sauce

Add the juice of one orange and quarter cup sherry to the
basic brown sauce (page 96). Serve with duck.

FRENCH DRESSING

YOU NEED

$1/4$ teaspoon any mustard
$1/2$ teaspoon white sugar
$1/4$ teaspoon salt
$1/4$ teaspoon paprika
4 tablespoons olive oil
2 tablespoons white vinegar
$1/2$ clove garlic crushed (optional)
$1/4$ tablespoon lemon juice

METHOD

Mix the mustard, sugar, salt, paprika and the oil until smooth.
Add vinegar, garlic and lemon juice. You can make a larger
quantity and store in bottle. Shake well before using.

CURRY DRESSING

Add half teaspoon curry powder to basic French dressing.

CHUTNEY DRESSING

Add half cup chutney to French dressing.

ROQUEFORT DRESSING

Add half cup crumbled Roquefort cheese to
basic French dressing.

MIXED HERB DRESSING

Add any fresh herbs chopped finely with one tablespoon of
Worcestershire sauce to basic French dressing (see previous
page for French dressing recipe).

THOUSAND ISLAND DRESSING

YOU NEED

$^1/_2$ cup mayonnaise

$^1/_4$ teaspoon chilli powder

1 tablespoon green capsicum chopped finely

6 stuffed olives chopped finely

1 tablespoon Worcestershire sauce

$^1/_4$ cup orange juice

$^1/_4$ cup tomato sauce

METHOD

Mix together. Add to basic French dressing (see page 101).

HOLLANDAISE SAUCE
EASY-STYLE

YOU NEED
2 egg yolks

1/4 lemon juice

1/4 teaspoon cayenne pepper.

METHOD
Add this to basic white sauce (page 96) stirring gently over low heat. Serve with asparagus or fish.

P.S. If you find Hollandaise sauce curdles, beat in three tablespoons boiling water until the sauce becomes smooth again.

HINT: If you find you have run out of flour for the sauce. Don't worry! Any white powdered packet soup will work (use the same quantity as the flour).

TARTARE SAUCE

YOU NEED
1 cup mayonnaise

1 tablespoon chives finely chopped

2 tablespoons capers finely chopped

1 pickled cucumber finely chopped

1 tablespoon fresh parsley finely chopped

METHOD
Mix all together and that's it!

CHAPTER SEVEN

WINE AND WHEN TO SERVE

Dad serves such wonderful red wines, full of flavour and texture. Only one problem, our guests get on the coffee table and dance after a couple of glasses! It's quite incredible, a few glasses of Dad's best rich red wine and there they are... up on the table. Tasting the, crimson juices is obviously very intoxicating. The temptation to jump up on the table is always too much for one of our friends, Murrie. He is a funny man with a devilish sense of humour, he makes us laugh. A glass or two of red and Murrie is up on the table tap dancing.

One particular time we thought it hysterical!
Mum didn't! Her coffee table was getting scratched and she was too polite to say anything, especially as a great time was being had by all. After a sensational show of tap dancing Mum decided that was it – no more dancing on any table unless he took his shoes off.

That coffee table had a strange hold on our tap dancing friend. One mad evening he was showing off his soft-sock-shuffle when he slipped and broke his arm. Mum felt awful. Friends now go down to Dad's wine cellar for the tastings on Mum's insistence. They obviously still have a ball as the cellar rings with singing and laughter. And Dad's fine reds which should be left for at least six more years seem to disappear before their time. And Murrie, arm in sling, still longingly looks at the coffee table.

Cheers!

from the cellar

COURSE	WINE	CHARACTERISTICS
Hors d'oeuvres	Chablis Rhine or Moselle	White wines – crisp, fresh and not as mellow as the wines served later in the dinner
Soup	Sherry (pale or dry) Madeira	White wines, as above or the heavier wines with their nutty flavour
Fish	White Bordeaux White Burgundy	White wines – not too sweet but light with a fragrant bouquet
Roasts & Red meats	Fine Clarets Burgundies	Red or white wines, a harmonious and subtle blending of bouquet, aroma, and body
Poultry	Full White Bordeaux Fine Burgundies Champagne	Light sparkling wine or flavoured white champagne

Cheese	*Fine Clarets or Red Burgundies*	
	Ports	
	Fine brown Sherry	*Not too sweet*
	Heavy vintage Madeiras	

Desserts	*Old full Sherry Madeiras*	*Moderately sweet*

Coffee	*Cognac*	*With the marvellous*
	Port	*bouquet that only*
		old age and breeding
		can give

CHAPTER EIGHT

AFRICAN

I've never written a proper diary – well, I mean put
every day down on paper. Sometimes, I wish I had kept
one but I knew Mum kept all my letters scribbled on
adventures abroad. Nevertheless, there are some
adventures I'll never forget.

The following happened to me when I returned to
Africa for the first time in ten years. I remember it in
minute detail. I was so excited at the thought of seeing
many of my old friends and travelling the game reserves
of Zimbabwe which had been my home for
so many years.

It was lovely seeing my friends again, nothing had
changed. We still laughed at the same jokes and shared
many new secrets. It was just like old times. But time
was short and sadly we had to part. I was really
disappointed as one of my friends was to travel with me
through Africa and at the last moment couldn't join
me. Well, I suppose I hadn't come this far to turn back
– so I decided to go it alone.

I journeyed through at least five African villages,
stopping a couple of times to share a meal. Moving on
and several hours later I found myself lost – completely
lost – miles from anywhere. I was chasing the light,
becoming afraid in my little jeep. Elephants crossed my
path and wildebeests threatened me with heads low.

corn on the cob

I was driving round in circles, one sand road looking like any other. When I had started out I had been so confident – my destination only a day away and here I was hopelessly lost and very hungry.

Out of the dark, I saw a man walking towards me. As he neared, I could see he had a ranger's uniform on. I can't describe my emotions... I laughed, cried and prayed he would guide me to my camp. I told him of my destination and although he had been on his way home to his own village he climbed aboard my jeep and directed me to camp.

Finally we drove into the camp and were met by a very worried game ranger who had been expecting me hours ago. Without another word he directed my new friend and I over to the boma (open fire encircled with bamboo
– a big outdoor kitchen) to share a meal of mufuta stew, mealie pap and merocha.
The rest of my stay passed wonderfully. My new friend told me long tales of the bush and filled my letters home with recipes from Africa. It was good to be back.

Here are some of those recipes.

Roasted Mealies
(Corn On The Cob)

YOU NEED

4 cobs

1 pinch salt

1 tablespoon oil

METHOD

Peel the leaves off the cob. Rub them all over with oil and salt and throw them into the dying embers of any fire for 15 minutes until golden brown.

I suppose these should be in the barbecue chapter but they are very African. There are meali fires around African railway stations. You find these in metal drums with holes punctured in the tops. The drums are filled with coals and the mealies are roasted on top and sold to passers-by.

MUFUTA STEW

Serves 5

YOU NEED

2 tablespoons oil
5 lamb forequarter chops trimmed
8 small onions whole
2 carrots chopped roughly
8 potatoes peeled, sliced thinly
3 cups water
pinch of salt and pepper
1 tablespoon curry powder

METHOD

Heat the oil in a large pot, add the lamb chops, cook over
moderate heat and let brown all over. Add the onions and
carrots and put the lid on the pot and cook gently.
Turn the chops and vegetables frequently.
When they become brown add a cup of water and replace the
lid and keep an eye on it as the water boils away.
Now add potatoes and two cups of water. Replace lid, cook
gently until chops are tender and falling away from the bone.
By this time you should have a really rich brown stew.
Lastly add the curry powder, salt and pepper.

This stew brings back memories.
It was served with mealie pap on the fateful night I got lost.
When you're hungry this is a feast for a king.
Oh, by the way, the mealie pap is actually corn on the cob
which has been dried and pounded to a rough floury
powder (see recipe next page).
Mufuta, the stew's name, means the fat one!

MEALI PAP
(CORN-MEAL POLENTA)

Serves 4

To me, many of these dishes used to have a mystique about them – their names alone scared me to death. Once I cooked them they turned out to be so easy it seemed ridiculous that I hadn't been cooking them for years.

YOU NEED

3 cups corn meal

3 cups water

$1/2$ teaspoon salt

METHOD

Bring salted water to boil in large saucepan and add corn meal slowly, stirring it as it thickens gradually.
Lower the heat and cook very gently until all the water has been absorbed and the mixture is crumbly.

Meali pap is to African people what potatoes are to the Irish. Well, that certainly sounds Irish!! In Africa, meali pap is whitish while corn meal – polenta is yellow but to me they taste the same. You can serve this with barbecues or you can eat it like porridge with milk and sugar.

HINT: The African people are not prone to heart attacks, or cancer. Maybe it's because they eat so much meali pap. Most health stores and supermarkets sell corn meal – polenta.

VENISON CASSEROLE
IN RED WINE

Serves 6

YOU NEED

1 leg venison

METHOD

Cut thick slices off the leg and add to the following marinade.

YOU NEED – VENISON MARINADE

2 cups red wine

$^1/_2$ cup vinegar

$^1/_4$ cup oil

1 teaspoon mixed spice

1 tablespoon nutmeg

1 teaspoon black peppercorn

A few bay leaves

METHOD

Preheat oven to 270°f.

Place slices of venison leg in casserole dish.

Mix all above ingredients together, pour marinade over the slices of venison and leave to marinate for half a day if possible. Cook in oven at 270°f for one hour.

The marinade will reduce in quantity and you will have a lovely sauce. Serve with mashed potatoes and green peas.

GOOSE WITH
APPLE STUFFING

Serves 12

YOU NEED
6kg goose

1 cup sherry

pinch salt and pepper

1 tablespoon ginger

*Combine together the following ingredients to
make the apple stuffing:*

2 cups apples chopped and cooked

2 tablespoons sugar

$1/4$ cup parsley chopped

$1/2$ onion finely chopped

2 cups breadcrumbs dry

$1/2$ cup carrot grated

pinch salt and pepper

1 tablespoon ginger

METHOD
Preheat oven to 300°f.

Wash and dry the goose (presuming that the innards have
been removed). Rub the goose inside with salt, pepper and
ginger combined. Place the goose in large roasting dish and
stuff with the apple stuffing. Prick the bird well with a fork to
allow the fat to run out. Pour a cup of sherry over goose.
Roast in 300°f oven for two hours. Lower heat to 250°f and
cook another three hours.

A REQUEST: Please don't go out and shoot any wild geese
unless there's nothing else to eat and you are
literally starving to death.

CHICKEN PERI PERI

Serves 6

YOU NEED

12 chicken pieces
$1/2$ cup flour
1 teaspoon thyme
1 teaspoon mixed spice seasoning
$1/4$ cup oil
$1/2$ tablespoon peri peri
(chilli powder will do)
$1/2$ teaspoon curry powder
$1/2$ cup vinegar white
1 clove garlic crushed
1 teaspoon brown sugar
1 onion grated
pinch salt and pepper

METHOD

Preheat oven to 300°f.
Roll the chicken pieces in flour, thyme and mixed spices.
Pour oil in pan and fry chicken pieces until golden brown.
Place the chicken in casserole dish. Then add the peri peri or
chilli powder and all the remaining ingredients. Bake in 300°f
oven for one hour or until the chicken is tender.

Serve with rice and salad.

ROAST DUCKLING WITH BRANDY AND ORANGE SAUCE

Serves 4

YOU NEED
1 duckling

1 tablespoon ginger

pinch salt and pepper

1 cup orange juice

$1/4$ cup brandy

$1/2$ cup water

1 tablespoon flour

METHOD
Preheat oven to 300°f.

Place duckling in roasting dish and rub ginger, salt and pepper
all over the duck. Then pour the orange juice and brandy
over it. Roast the duckling until brown all over while
spooning its juices frequently over the bird. Also turn the
duck on all sides. You may need to add a little more liquid.
I think you've got enough brandy so add a splash of water.
When the duck is done, remove from roasting dish
and keep warm.

Make the gravy by putting the roasting pan on the top of the
stove and add a little water to the sediment and boil while
adding that tablespoon of flour. Mix well and if the gravy is
too thick add more water. Then strain and keep hot.

Serve with wild rice.

aronson

BOBOTIE

Serves 6

YOU NEED
1 cup water
2 thick slices bread
2 tablespoons butter
2 onions sliced finely
1 tablespoon chutney
1 tablespoon curry powder
$1/4$ cup lemon juice
pinch salt and pepper
1 $1/2$ kg minced beef
2 eggs beaten

METHOD
Preheat oven to 250°f.
Soak bread in water and mash with fork. Melt butter in pan
and fry onions until soft. Then add the chutney, curry
powder, mashed bread, lemon juice, seasoning, minced beef
and half of the beaten eggs. Pour mixture into greased pie tin.
Bake in oven at 250°f for half an hour. add the rest of the egg
to the pie and cook another half hour.
Serve with rice and hot chutney.

African Sweet Potatoes

Serves 6

YOU NEED

4 sweet potatoes

3 tablespoons butter

1 cinnamon stick

2 tablespoons brown sugar

pinch salt and pepper

1 cup water

METHOD

Peel and slice the potato thinly into a saucepan and add all the other ingredients. Let the potatoes cook very gently until water has boiled away. Remove cinnamon stick and let cook until the potatoes turn brown.

MELK TERT

Serves 8

YOU NEED – SHORTCRUST PASTRY

1 $\frac{1}{2}$ cups self-raising flour

pinch salt

$\frac{1}{2}$ cup butter

$\frac{1}{4}$ cup cold water

METHOD

Put flour in mixing bowl, add the salt and cut the butter into
tiny pieces. Rub this together with your fingers very lightly
until they form into crumbs. Add the cold water a little at a
time, mixing to form a stiff dough.

Chill dough before rolling out.

When ready to make the pie, roll the pastry out on a floured
board. Handle the pastry as little possible as this keeps it light.
See over page for filling.

HINT: You can buy really good shortcrust pastry in case you
haven't time to make it.

YOU NEED – FILLING

2 cups milk

2 tablespoons cornflour

2 tablespoons butter

2 tablespoons sugar

dash of vanilla

2 egg yolks

1 teaspoon cinnamon

METHOD

Preheat oven to 300°f.

Grease a pie dish and line with pastry. Mix cornflour in small bowl with three tablespoons of milk (leave aside). Put the rest of milk in sauce pan with the butter and sugar and cook very slowly until milk begins to bubble. Add a dash of vanilla. Pour in cornflour paste and cook very gently stirring all the time until the mixture thickens. Add beaten egg yolks and stir through. Remove from heat and pour into pie shell. Bake at 300°f for 30 minutes until the pastry is golden brown and filling has set. Allow to cool then sprinkle with cinnamon.

CHAPTER NINE

QUICK VEGETARIAN

A letter from Mum to my brother who was travelling Europe... indulging.

Hello Darling!

I miss saying that every time you bursted through the door at Willow Wild Road. I'm sitting in the garden and I'm not leaving till I've written this overdue letter. It's 5.30 on Thursday afternoon and I'm catching the last rays of the setting sun.

Wonderful to hear all your news and amazed to hear you're thinking of becoming a vegetarian. Do you remember my friend Docrett. My dear friend? Well, she's vegetarian and boy can she cook – she whips up all kinds of delights. Every meal a surprise. You name it. Anyway, I know you love cooking so I've enclosed her vegetable samosa and her vegetable souffle recipes. Both are my favourites and they're so easy to make.

Your father took me to the Clareville beach house last weekend. A quick trip, arriving late Friday night and leaving again at 7pm Sunday, but still it was like a little holiday. The sun shone steadily and I got sunburnt knees. Well my darling, lovely scribbling to you.

All my love and more

Mum

VEGETABLE SAMOSAS

Makes 20

YOU NEED – FILLING

4 large potatoes partially cooked

1 cup carrots

2 tablespoons butter

1 cup peas

1 onion sliced

$1/2$ teaspoon chilli powder

pinch of salt

YOU NEED – PASTRY

3 cups plain flour

1 teaspoon baking powder

pinch of salt

1 cup yoghurt

oil for frying

METHOD – FILLING

Boil the peas and carrots until soft, strain and put to one side.
Slice potatoes. Melt the butter in a saucepan and toss in the
onion, cook until soft and brown. Add the sliced potatoes and
cook a little. Next, add the cooked peas, chilli powder and
salt. Close the lid and allow to cook gently (don't add water).
When potatoes are soft, remove and cool.

See page 126 for pastry method.

handful of chillis

METHOD – PASTRY

Mix flour, baking powder, salt, yogurt and add as much water as necessary to form a stiff pastry. Mix with hands to combine pastry. Turn dough out onto a floured board. Knead pastry until smooth and elastic. Place in a bowl, cover and let stand for an hour. Now roll out and cut into rounds with lip (edge) of cup.Place a little of the vegetables in the centre of each round, moisten the edges with water and fold over in the form of a triangle. Seal all joins very carefully. Have the hot oil in a frying pan ready to go. Carefully place the samosa in – a few at a time - cooking both sides to a beautiful golden brown, approximately one minute each.
Drain on absorbent paper, newspaper is perfect.

YOGHURT AND CUMIN DIP

This dip is a must with samosas, otherwise you might
find them a bit dry.

YOU NEED
1 cup yoghurt natural
1 clove garlic crushed
$^1/_4$ cup cream
1 teaspoon fresh dill chopped finely
$^1/_2$ teaspoon cumin

METHOD
Mix all ingredients together and chill.

POLENTA BAKE

Serves 4

YOU NEED

1 small onion chopped finely
2 tablespoons butter
1 zuccini peeled and chopped
1 red capsicum (for colour) chopped finely
1 handful of sliced mushrooms
(the size of your hand doesn't matter)
a small bunch of parsley chopped finely
1 cup Polenta
1 cup wholemeal self raising flour
1 level teaspoon of sodium bicarbonate
$1/2$ cup cheddar cheese and $1/2$ cup of
roughly grated parmesan cheese
decent pinch of salt and black pepper
1 cup buttermilk (if you don't have
buttermilk add a splash of vinegar to fresh
milk, this makes it go sour)

METHOD

Preheat the oven to 220°f.
Line a 22cm square baking dish (or something roughly
that size) with grease-proof paper or Glad Bake paper if
you've got it. It will still work if you don't have paper, just
brush the dish with melted butter and then dust with flour.

Fry onion in pan with butter until soft, add the chopped
zuccini and capsicum, cook for a minute. Now add the
mushrooms and parsley, mix together and then take off the
heat and leave to one side for the moment.

In a large bowl add wholemeal self raising flour, polenta,
sodium bicarbonate, cheese, salt and pepper.
Stir in the buttermilk and then grab those vegetables you took
off the heat and mix the lot together. Pour this into the
prepared baking dish and bake at 220°f for 35 minutes, to
check if cooked pierce with skewer or knife and if it comes
out clean it's cooked.

SAUCE

See page 229 for a delicious tomato and onion sauce – a must
with Polenta Bake.

VEGETARIAN SOUFFLE

Serves 6

YOU NEED

4 tablespoons butter

1 tablespoon onion chopped finely

4 tablespoons flour

1 teaspoon rosemary fresh or dried

1 cup water

1 vegetable stock cube

1 1/2 cups of mixed vegetables (green peas,
mushrooms, zuccini, carrots and
broccoli florets cooked)

4 eggs separated

1 cup cream

NOTE: Souffles are traditionally difficult to make.
This is easy but take your time and read the method
through carefully.

METHOD

Preheat oven to 370°f.

Melt butter in fry pan, add onion and cook until soft. Stir in
flour and rosemary. Add water and stock cube, cook until
thickened. Now add the vegetables, mix gently, add the yolk
of eggs and cream and cook very slowly for 30 seconds. Let
the mixture cool a little. While it's cooling quickly beat your
egg whites - if you want to make sure the egg whites are
ready, turn the bowl you mixed them in upside-down. If the
egg stays put, it's stiff enough!! Now fold the beaten egg
whites into the mixture very gently. Pour into buttered
baking dish and bake in oven at 370°f until golden brown on
top and firm. Cooking time 15 minutes.

Serve immediately.

CURRIED EGG PLANT

Serves 4

YOU NEED

2 tablespoons olive oil

2 onions sliced thinly

2 cloves garlic crushed

1 teaspoon curry powder

pinch salt

2 cups natural yogurt

$1/2$ teaspoon ginger

$1/2$ teaspoon coriander powder

1 tablespoon brown sugar

3 egg plants slice lengthwise

$1/2$ cup water

1 tablespoon hot chutney

METHOD

Fry onion and garlic in oil until soft. Add the curry powder,
salt and stir. Add the yogurt, mix with the ginger, coriander
and sugar, add this to the onions.
Cook gently until the mixture is a thick paste.
Add the water, egg plant and chutney cook until soft.
Cooking time 25 minutes and serve with rice.

VEGETABLE PIE

Serves 8

YOU NEED

3 large potatoes chopped
2 large onions chopped
4 medium carrots chopped
1 cup peas (cooked)
1 cup tinned kidney beans
1 cup tinned tomatoes
$1/4$ cup cheddar cheese grated
pinch of salt
pinch of pepper
1 vegetable stock cube
1 sheet puff pastry

METHOD

Preheat oven 450°f.
Put all the fresh vegetables into a pot of boiling water and cook for ten minutes. Drain off the water add tinned tomatoes, kidney beans, seasonings and stock cube. Mix all the ingredients together, sprinkle with cheese and put into an oven-proof dish. Cover with puff pastry.
Bake in oven for 25 minutes.

POTATO PUFFS

Serves 4

YOU NEED

1 $1/2$ cups mashed potato
1 $1/2$ teaspoons baking powder
$1/2$ cup flour
salt and pepper to taste
1 egg
chives chopped finely

METHOD

Mix all the above ingredients together.
Drop tablespoons into hot oil. When golden remove from fat
and drain on absorbent paper. Ready!

HINT: If you like reading in the bath and you
wear glasses then rub a slice of potato on the lenses and this
stops them steaming up.

SAVOURY RICE

Serves 4

YOU NEED
1 cup white rice
$1^1/_2$ cups water
pinch of salt
2 tablespoons butter
1 cup finely chopped onions
1 cup finely chopped capsicum
handful of chopped mushrooms
$^1/_2$ bunch finely chopped chives
2 eggs

METHOD
Bring rice to boil in pot of salted water and then simmer for
15 minutes. Remove from heat, drain and leave aside.

In a fry pan melt butter, add the onions and cook until soft.
Add capsicum, mushroom, and chives. Cook gently for 10
minutes. Now break eggs into this mixture, allow to cook
until firm and then chop up with the other ingredients.
Now toss the rice into the pan and mix through.
Voila!

BAKED POTATOES WITH CHIVES, SOUR CREAM AND PECANS

Serves 4

YOU NEED

4 large potatoes

1 teaspoon salt

$^1/_2$ cup sour cream

2 tablespoons fresh chives

$^1/_2$ cup pecan nuts

pinch of salt and pepper

METHOD

Preheat oven to 450°f.

Wash and dry potatoes, rub salt all over them and
pop into the oven. Ignore for 40 minutes or until potatoes
are tender (depending on size).

Remove from oven, cut in half and top with sour cream,
pecans, chives and sprinkle with salt and pepper.

Baked Potatoes
With Cheese, Mushroom
And Onion

Serves 4

YOU NEED
4 large potatoes
$^1/_2$ cup cheddar cheese grated
1 teaspoon salt
$^1/_2$ cup onion grated
1 cup mushrooms

METHOD
Preheat oven to 450°f.
Wash and dry potatoes. Rub with salt and throw in the oven
for 40 minutes. Remove from oven and cut in half. Top with
mixture of onion, cheese and mushroom and place under a
hot grill for five minutes or until golden brown.

P.S. These potatoes are a great standby for unexpected
vegetarian guests.

MOUSSAKA

Serves 8

YOU NEED
4 large eggplants (aubergines)
2 tablespoons butter
1 teaspoon salt
1 1/2 cups cheddar cheese grated
2 cups white sauce
2 cups Napoli sauce (see page 100) — if you
want to take a shortcut you can always use
Paul Newmans bolognese sauce instead, or
any ready-made bolognese sauce. Easy to
find at all supermarkets.

NOTE: See page 96 and page 100 for tomato and white
sauces recipes

METHOD
Preheat oven to 350°f.
Cut eggplants into long strips. Place on plate and sprinkle with
salt leave to drain on the plate for ten minutes. Melt butter on
fry pan and fry the eggplant until soft. Layer eggplant in
bottom of casserole dish and pour a layer of tomato sauce and
then a layer of white sauce. Repeat this until eggplant and
sauces are used up, layer upon layer. Sprinkle cheese over the
top and bake in the oven at 350°f for 30 minutes.

P.S. This is a super dish served with Greek salad.

HINT: Never cut a lettuce with a knife but break it with
your hands. It tastes better, or so they say!

NACHOS WITH GUACAMOLE

Serves 4

YOU NEED – FOR NACHOS
3 tablespoons butter
1 onion finely chopped
1 clove garlic crushed
$^{1}/_{2}$ teaspoon chilli powder
1 teaspoon paprika
2 cups tinned tomatoes chopped
2 cups tinned kidney beans drained
3 cups corn chips

METHOD
Melt butter in fry pan. Add onion and garlic, cook until soft.
Now add chilli, paprika and tomatoes. Don't forget the
kidney beans, they're next.
Cook gently until mixture has thickened. Arrange corn chips
on plate, pour kidney bean mixture into centre of corn chips
and add a good dollop of guacamole.
Top with grated cheese and pop under grill.

Guacamole recipe next page.

GUACAMOLE

YOU NEED

2 avocado's ripe

1 cup soft cream cheese

$1/2$ cup plain yogurt

$1/4$ cup lemon juice

6 drops tabasco sauce

METHOD

Mix all the ingredients together.
Serve on top of Nachos.

CHAPTER TEN

ITALIAN

We had these Italian friends who taught Mum all she
knows about pasta. Our friends the Nucci's had such
style and I loved being with them.
I felt part of the family. They wanted to adopt me.
My Mum says she doesn't know why because only a
Mother could love me.

Saturday lunches were always special at the Nucci's,
nothing can quite compare (maybe Mum's breakfasts). I
used to call him Papa Nucci. I loved him. Papa Nucci
used to spend the whole Saturday morning preparing
lunch. He brought the food onto the table with a
flourish and sat at the head surrounded with family and
friends – 20 to 30 people at a time.
He tossed the pasta, and poured the wine (it was never
unusual for the children to have a drop of red with
their meal like most Italian children.
Of course, it was mixed with water!).

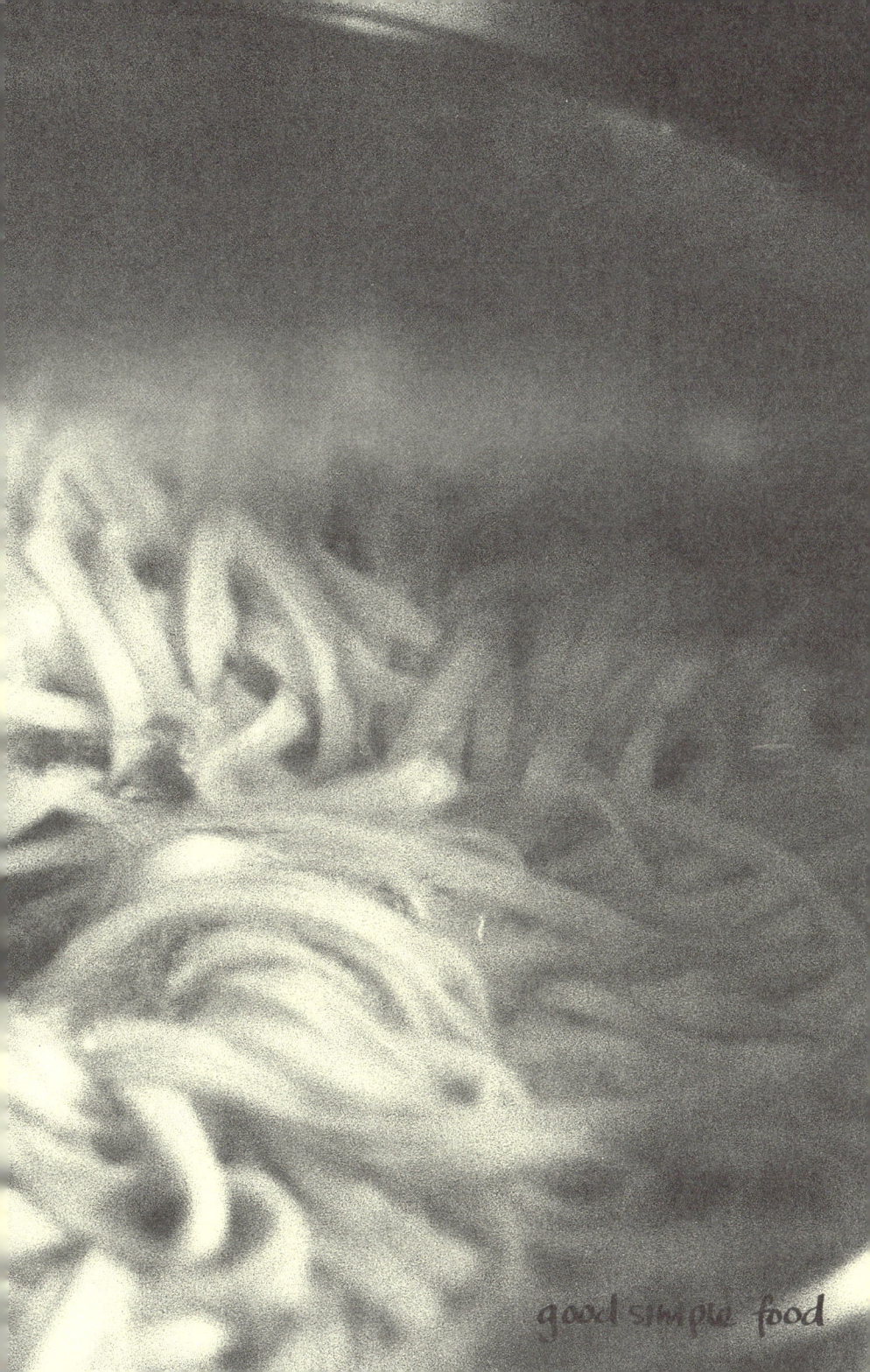

good simple food

It was such a happy time in my life and I was sad when we moved away. I missed them, the laughter, the song and the pasta. Mama Nucci used to say "pasta, sauce and song belong together". My darling Mum tried to fill the gap when we moved. Well, she had most of Papa Nucci's recipes and she had a lot of laughter but the song... Mum's repertoire was limited and on pasta day we could hear 'O Sol Mia' at least ten times. Even the dog would look quite depressed. Mum eventually realised opera wasn't really necessary to make a good pasta just a good spirit.

PAPA NUCCI'S
NEOPOLITANA PASTA

Serves 6

YOU NEED

5 fresh tomatoes peeled and chopped

2 tablespoons Italian olive oil

$1/2$ onion chopped finely

1 clove garlic crushed

6 rashers bacon without rind and chopped

handful of mushrooms sliced finely

3 cups tinned peeled Italian tomatoes
chopped

$1/4$ cup fresh basil chopped (if you can't get
any fresh basil, dried will be fine)

$1/2$ cup red wine

pinch of salt

2 pinches of pepper

1 tablespoon tomato paste

HINT: Do try and use Italian olive oil and Italian peeled
tomatoes as they are loaded with lots more flavour. However,
if you haven't got any Italian (ha, ha) at hand or can't find it
in the deli any olive oil and peeled tomatoes will still turn out
a delicious Neopolitana sauce.
Method over page.

METHOD

Submerge fresh tomatoes in boiling water (and let them stand while you prepare the sauce) until skin comes away easily. Put olive oil in deep fry pan, toss in onion and garlic and fry until soft (don't let it burn). Add the bacon and let cook for three minutes. Next, add the mushrooms and fresh, peeled tomatoes. Stir and cook for three minutes, now add tinned tomatoes and fresh basil, salt and pepper. Don't forget a tablespoon of tomato paste and lastly the red wine.

Cover and let cook and bubble gently for a couple of hours for flavours to come through. If it looks like it's evaporating and losing all its moisture, simply add some more red wine. This is best served with penne as all the lovely juices can flow into the noodle shape and trap the flavours.

PAPA NUCCI'S METHOD FOR COOKING PASTA

Boil water in large pot with sprinkle of salt and a drop of olive oil (this stops the pasta sticking together). Add spaghetti, gradually loosening it with a fork. Cook until tender. You can check by biting through and if there is any white marking inside it is not ready. Or, one test we use all the time is to throw it up onto the ceiling, if it sticks it is ready! Drain well. Put spaghetti onto serving dish, toss in a tablespoon of butter and a sprinkling of pepper. Serve hot.

__HINT:__ Pasta, like all things good, is best when eaten as simply as possible. The sauce should not drown but lightly coat. The trick is to add the sauce to the pasta before serving and to eat it as soon as possible with loads of roughly grated parmesan cheese. Buon Appetite!

YOU NEED

12 large mushrooms stems removed

2 zucchinis cut in long strips

1 cucumber cut in long strips

6 spring onions or shallots trimmed

$1/2$ bulb fennel chopped

1 bunch asparagus spears cooked

1 egg plant thinly sliced

6 slices prosciutto

6 slices salami

small round of goats cheese

jar of black olives

YOU NEED – FOR MARINADE

$1/4$ cup Italian olive oil

$1/2$ cup fresh lemon juice

1 clove garlic crushed

pinch of salt and black pepper crushed

METHOD

Mix the marinade ingredients together in a big bowl. Toss in
all the prepared vegetables and let stand for a few hours
Remove from the marinade ready for antipasta plate. To this,
add slices of prosciutto, salami, goats cheese and black olives.
Drizzle with left over marinade and that's it.
Can you believe it's as simple as that?

TOMATO-FILLED PESTO
AND SPINACH

Serves 4

YOU NEED

2 tablespoons Italian olive oil

2 cups fresh basil chopped

$3/4$ cup parmesan cheese grated

1 clove garlic

4 tablespoons pine nuts

4 tablespoons soft butter

2 cups spinach chopped and cooked

$1/4$ cup goats cheese sliced

2 medium-sized ripe tomatoes

2 tablespoons lemon juice

METHOD

Place basil, parmesan cheese, garlic, pine nuts and lemon juice in blender with olive oil. Blend until a thick paste and that's your pesto. Remove the mixture to a bowl and beat in the butter. Add the spinach and few pieces of goats cheese.
Cut medium-sized tomatoes in half, scoop out centre of tomato and mix in with spinach mixture.
Spoon back into tomato and place under a hot grill until heated through and a touch crispy on top.

P.S. If you want to cheat a little you can buy some wonderfully delicious pesto's from the deli.

HINT: Never use herbs and spices to the extent that they overpower the natural flavour of food.

ITALIAN BREAD

YOU NEED

1 3/4 cups of sour milk (just add a little
vinegar to milk if you don't have any)
2 cups of self-raising flour
good pinch salt

METHOD

Preheat oven to 350°f.
Place flour and salt in mixing bowl, add sour milk and slowly
mix well with a wooden spoon. Empty mixture into a greased
loaf tin. Bake in middle of oven for one hour.

HINT: Fresh bread will cut more easily with a heated knife.

HERB BREAD

YOU NEED

5 cups self-raising flour

1 cup wholemeal flour

3 tablespoons of each: fresh parsley, chives,

basil and rosemary or any other fresh herbs

you wish to use

$1/2$ teaspoon garlic crushed (optional)

3 tablespoons soft brown sugar

2 cups sour milk with 1 beaten egg

$1/4$ cup sesame seeds

METHOD

Preheat oven to 350°f.

Mix all dry ingredients together except the sesame seeds, stir
in the sour milk and beaten egg. This should be quite a stiff
dough. Grease and sprinkle flour in a 25cm round bread or
cake tin. Sprinkle sesame seeds on the top and bake at
350°f for one hour.

To test if ready put a dry knife through the centre – if it
comes out perfectly clean the bread is done. Eat straight from
the oven and have lashings of butter with it.

Goat's Cheese And Tomato Pizza

Serves 8

YOU NEED – PIZZA BASE

1 tablespoon yeast

1 tablespoon sugar

1 cup warm water

2 $1/2$ cups plain flour

pinch of salt

3 tablespoons Italian olive oil

METHOD

Mix yeast and sugar together in small bowl, add warm water
and let this stand until bubbles appear on the surface.
In the meantime, combine flour and salt in another bowl, add
olive oil and then the yeast mixture that you made earlier.
Mix to a firm dough. Turn out onto a floured board and
knead until dough is quite elastic. Put dough back in bowl,
cover with a damp tea towel and let stand for 35 minutes.
Roll out dough to fit 20cm pizza pan.
By the way, if you can't be bothered making the pizza base
you can buy them. I've seen really good substitute bases in
deli's and supermarkets – worth a try!

YOU NEED – FOR TOPPING

2 tablespoons Italian olive oil

$1/2$ onion grated roughly

1 clove garlic crushed

1 cup tinned peeled tomatoes chopped

1 teaspoon fresh chopped basil

1 teaspoon pesto (optional)

1 cup sliced goats cheese

$1/2$ cup finely sliced black olives

METHOD

Preheat oven to 350°f.

Heat oil in fry pan and add grated onion. Cook gently, until soft then add crushed garlic, stir for a few seconds. Add tomatoes with liquid and stir constantly. Now add fresh basil and pesto, bring to boil and then let cook slowly for 30 minutes. It should be a lovely thick sauce. Allow sauce to cool. Spread sauce over pizza base as much or as little as you prefer. Top with thick slices of goat's cheese and slivers of black olives. Drizzle a little olive oil over top of cheese, this keeps it from drying out. Bake in oven at 350°f for 15 minutes until crust is a lovely golden brown.

Spaghetti Bolognese

Serves 8

YOU NEED
1 packet spaghetti (any kind)
lots of parmesan cheese grated

YOU NEED – BOLOGNESE SAUCE
3 tablespoons olive oil or butter
1 large onion chopped
1 rasher bacon chopped (optional)
1 clove garlic crushed
$1/2$ kg best beef mince
2 cups tinned tomatoes
1 cup tomato puree
2 tablespoons tomato paste
1 small cup red wine
2 cups water
$1/2$ teaspoon nutmeg

METHOD
Heat oil or butter in big pot and add the onion, bacon and
cook gently for two minutes. Then add finely crushed garlic.
Add beef mince to the onion mixture and stir the meat until it
separates and browns slightly. Now add roughly chopped
tomatoes and juice, tomato puree and tomato paste.
Don't forget the red wine and two cups of water. Let the
mixture simmer for approximately 45 minutes then add
nutmeg. You should now have a red rich meaty sauce.
Bolognese has to be really rich in tomato otherwise it's not
true Bolognese and sprinkled with healthy amounts of
parmesan cheese, so Mum says!!
See page 145 for how to cook spaghetti.

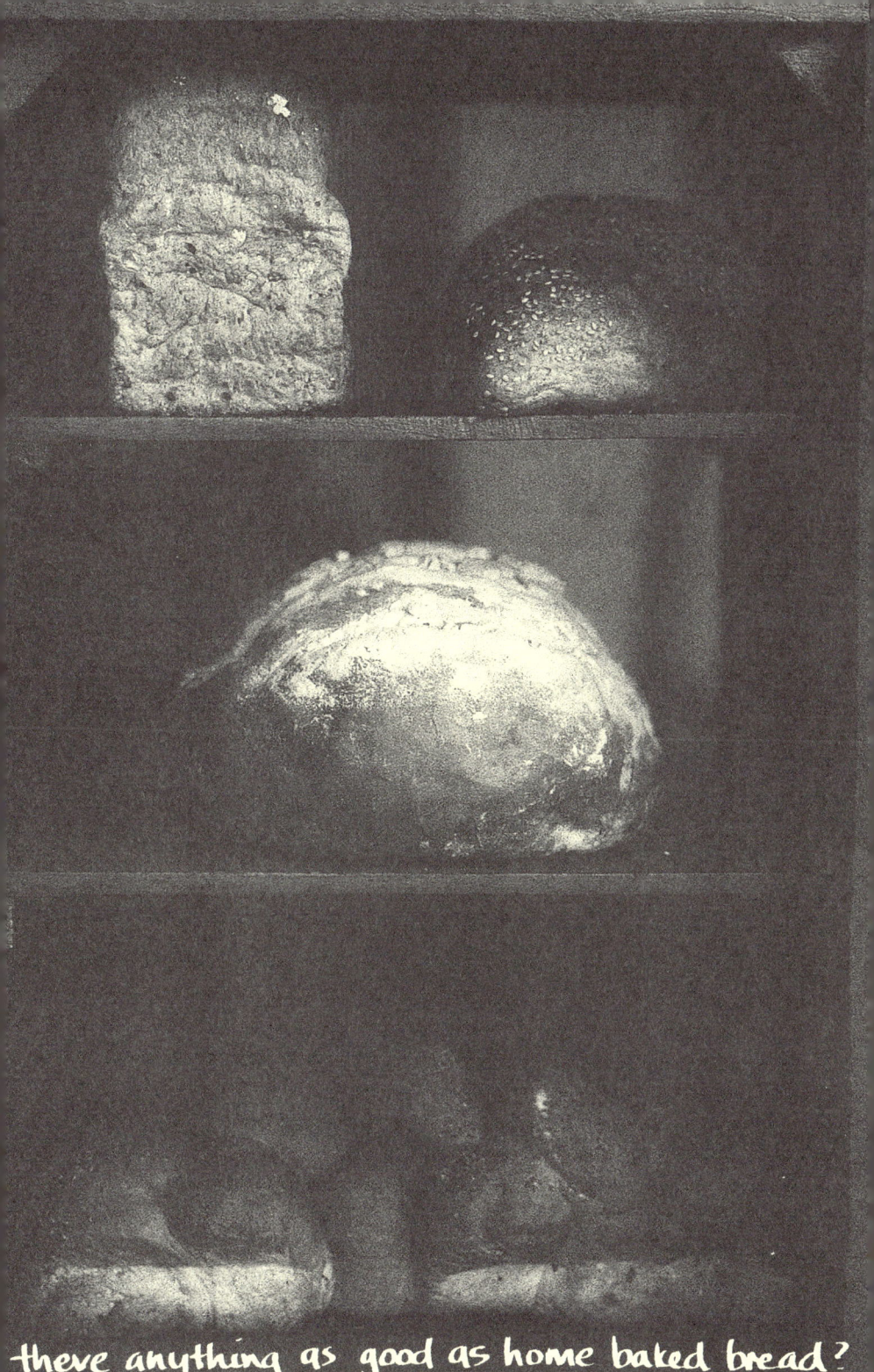

there anything as good as home baked bread?

FETTUCINE JO-JO

Serves 8

YOU NEED

1 tablespoon butter

8 rashers bacon chopped

$^1/_4$ cup grated onion

10 large mushrooms

2 cups cheese sauce (see page 98)

1 tablespoon pesto

2 packets dry fettucine

METHOD

Melt butter in saucepan and fry bacon with onions.
Cook gently for three to four minutes add sliced mushrooms,
cheese sauce (see page 98) and pesto. Gently put the fettucine
into a large pot of rapidly boiling salted water add a drop of
olive oil to the water and gently separate with a fork,this keeps
it from sticking together. When cooked drain well. Mum
always runs cold water over the pasta which seems to keep it
from going gluggy. Before serving pop the fettucine back into
boiling water for one minute.

Macaroni Pie
With Bacon, Tomato
And Cheese

YOU NEED

4 cups macaroni cooked

6 rashers bacon chopped

1 large onion sliced thinly

4 cups cheese sauce (see page 98)

2 large tomatoes sliced

1 cup grated cheddar cheese

METHOD

Cook macaroni in rapidly boiling water for 15 minutes. When cooked drain off the water. Fry chopped bacon lightly. Fry onions in bacon's fat until soft. Add the cheese sauce, onions, bacon, macaroni and stir through. Turn into oven-proof dish and arrange slices of tomato and sprinkle grated cheese on top. Warm through in oven then pop under grill.

LASAGNE

Serves 6

YOU NEED

2 tablespoons Italian olive oil

$^3/4$ kg best beef mince

1 large onion chopped finely

1 $^1/2$ cup tinned peeled tomatoes

1 beef stock cube crumbled

1 clove garlic crushed

1 tablespoon pesto

1 cup sliced mushrooms

2 tablespoons tomato paste

1 pinch salt and pepper

1 large pack instant lasagne sheets

1 medium-sized jug cheese sauce
(see page 98)

$^1/4$ cup parmesan cheese grated

$^1/4$ cup cheddar cheese grated

2 fresh tomatoes sliced

See over page for method.

MEAT SAUCE METHOD

Preheat oven to 350°f.

Heat oil in large pot. Add mince and cook until slightly brown. Add chopped onion and cook for three minutes. Throw in peeled tomatoes which have been roughly chopped plus juice from can, stock cube, crushed garlic, pesto, mushrooms, tomato paste, salt and pepper. Bring gently to boil and simmer for 30 minutes or until liquid has reduced. You can buy instant lasagne sheets from any supermarket.

No pre-cooking required just use lasagne sheets straight from packet.

Oil large flat square casserole and cover the base with layer of meat sauce. Then arrange layer of lasagne sheets and cover with cheese sauce. Repeat layers of meat sauce, lasagne, cheese sauce until all the sheets are used up. Cover the top layer of lasagne with both sauces. Arrange slices of tomato and sprinkle parmesan and cheddar cheese on top.

Bake in moderate oven 350°f until golden brown for approximately 40 minutes. Serve Lasagne with a great Italian salad and crusty garlic or herb bread.

RATATOUILLE

Serves 8

YOU NEED

$^1/_2$ cup Italian olive oil

2 cloves garlic crushed

2 onions

2 eggplants (aubergine)

2 tablespoons plain flour

2 red capsicums seeded

2 green capsicums seeded

2 zucchinis

4 large tomatoes

1 tablespoons tomato paste

$^1/_4$ cup white wine

NOTE: All the above vegetables should be chopped chunky style

METHOD

Heat oil in deep fry pan, add onion and garlic, cook gently until soft. Toss both sides of the egg plant pieces in flour and add to the fry pan, cooking gently for five minutes (keep the heat low) and toss in the capsicums and zucchinis cooking for a few minutes. Next, add the tomatoes, the tomato paste and wine. Put a lid on the fry pan or cover with foil, cook gently for 15 minutes.

P.S. I love ratatouille, it's one of my favourite Italian dishes – lovely served hot or cold in a colourful bowl.

HINT: Peel onions under cold water to prevent tears.

PENNE WITH PROSCIUTTO
AND BLUE VEIN CHEESE

Serves 4

Penne looks a bit like macaroni but it's thinner.
This is a great recipe.

YOU NEED
1 packet penne

3 slices prosciutto cut thickly

1 $^1/_2$ cups peas – cook in boiling water
till tender

1 tablespoon butter

2 tablespoons packet mushroom soup

$^1/_4$ teaspoon cracked black pepper

1 cup white wine

$^1/_2$ cup cream

1 cup blue vein cheese crumbled

PREPARATION
Cook penne in rapidly boiling water for 15 minutes. When
cooked drain off the water. Chop prosciutto into pieces, drain
the green peas and keep warm.

SAUCE METHOD
Melt butter in saucepan, add two tablespoons mushroom soup
from a packet and blend together over low heat. Add black
pepper and wine, simmer gently for few minutes then add
cream and blue vein cheese.

Mix peas and prosciutto with penne and serve on individual
plates with oodles of blue vein sauce.

CHAPTER ELEVEN

Puddings
Hot And Cold

Mum was just saying "Don't be an old meanie" about
sharing your favourite recipes. There's not a recipe in
the world that can't be found somewhere.
Anyway, no two cooks ever cook the same.

One recipe which Mum battled to get was Sticky
Toffee Pudding (bet you haven't got it and if you have,
Mum must have given it to you!)
Well, Mum spent many hours over the hot stove trying
to invent and unravel the mystery of this mouth-
watering pudding. There she stood - mixing, beating
and baking while everyone would come in to see if her
concoction was right, tasting this and that.

Finally, she won and now I honestly believe Mum
makes it better than all the professionals. So here it is
and I hope you enjoy it as much as all our friends do.

With love from Mum.

apples off the tree

TILLY'S APPLE CRUST PIE

YOU NEED

short crust pastry (see page 121)

6 cooking apples

(ask your green grocer or you can get away

with using tinned apples if you haven't time)

1/4 cup lemon juice

1 cup sugar

3 tablespoons flour

1/4 teaspoon cloves

1/2 teaspoon nutmeg

1/4 teaspoon all spice

3/4 cup cream

METHOD

Preheat oven 400°f.

Peel apples and slice thinly. Sprinkle with lemon juice.
Combine sugar, flour, cloves, nutmeg and all spice in mixing
bowl and toss in the apples. Mix well. Now add the cream.
Put this mixture into deep oven-proof dish.

Roll out enough pastry to fit over dish. Brush the top of
pastry with a little milk. Cut off any excess pastry around the
edges and seal by pressing with the back of a spoon.
Bake in 400°f oven for 45 minutes.

Serve with ladles of thick cream or ice-cream.

RHONA'S BLINTZES

Makes 20

YOU NEED

3 eggs

1 cup water

1 cup milk

1 tablespoon oil

1 $^1/_2$ cups plain flour

pinch salt

METHOD – FOR BATTER

Beat eggs, milk and water. Add oil and mix well. Add flour, salt and beat until really smooth. Heat a small frying or crepe pan (should be quite hot) and grease lightly with oil. Pour a very thin layer of batter covering the bottom of the pan. Cook until golden then turn over and cook for a second or so on the other side. Repeat until all the batter mixture has been used and stack them one on top of the other, this keeps them moist. Now for the filling, see over page.

YOU NEED – FOR FILLING
1 egg

2 cups soft cream cheese

2 tablespoons sour cream

$^1/_2$ cup sultanas

2 teaspoons cinnamon

3 tablespoons castor sugar

2 tablespoons butter melted

METHOD
Preheat oven to 250°f.

Mix all ingredients (except for butter) until smooth. Place a good tablespoon in the centre of each blintz. Wrap it up like a little parcel and put them side by side in a well-greased dish. Drizzle a bit of melted butter over the top of the blintzes. Bake at 250°f for about 20 minutes.

This is a very special recipe. I hold it dear to my heart. It belonged to my dear friend Rhona Jacobs. We shared many a recipe, many a laugh and believe me, many a tear. Thanks Rho.

CHOCOLATE MARQUIS

YOU NEED

1 cup butter

$^3/4$ cup castor sugar

$^3/4$ cup of cocoa powder

6 egg yolks beaten

$^3/4$ cup melted chocolate buttons

2 cups thickened cream

2 tablespoons of gelatine disolved in 2
tablespoons of boiling water

METHOD

Mix butter, castor sugar and cocoa together. Add egg yolks,
gently beat and add melted chocolate. Mix well. Slowly beat in
cream then add gelatine. Spoon mixture into lightly buttered
long glass dish. Place in refrigerator to set. When set and ready to
serve, warm the bottom of the dish to free the pudding. To
warm put the dish in hot water for a few seconds.

Serve with Strawbery Puree.

STRAWBERRY PUREE

YOU NEED

1 punnet strawberries

1 punnet black berries

1 tablespoon castor sugar

1 dash Tia Maria liqueur

METHOD

Pop all the ingredients into a blender and blend until smooth.
Serve slices of chocolate marquis on a bed of this sumptious
strawberry puree. Decorate with freshly picked mint.

ROSH'S PLUM TART

YOU NEED

6 tablespoons butter

2 tablespoons castor sugar

2 tablespoons oil

1 egg beaten

splash vanilla

2 cups self-raising flour

1 teaspoon baking powder

3 cups fresh plums cooked and drained

(You can of course use tinned. Oh, don't

forget to take the stones out of plums!)

$^1/_4$ cup castor sugar

METHOD

Preheat oven to 300°f.

Cream butter and castor sugar together in bowl and add oil.
Stir in egg, splash of vanilla then add flour and baking powder.
Mix together and divide the dough in two. Place in freezer for
one hour until firm. Grease a 22cm pie dish and grate one half
of dough into the dish covering the base and sides.
Now add the plums and a quarter cup of castor sugar.
Grate remaining dough over top of plums. Bake at 300°f for
30-40 minutes until golden brown.

P.S. You can use tinned apples instead of plums. If you have
time to use fresh cooked fruit then do as it's truly delicious.

STICKY TOFFEE DATE PUDDING WITH TOFFEE SAUCE

Serves 10

YOU NEED

2 $\frac{1}{2}$ cups chopped dates

2 cups water

1 heaped teaspoon bi-carbonate soda

generous splash vanilla

8 tablespoons soft butter

$\frac{3}{4}$ cup castor sugar

3 eggs

1 $\frac{3}{4}$ cups self-raising flour

METHOD

Preheat oven at 350°f.

Prepare dish for pudding before taking another step. Brush a 20cm baking dish with oil or even better line the dish with grease proof paper or Glad Bake paper – now you're ready!

Put dates and water in saucepan and bring to boil.

Add bi-carbonate of soda, stir for a minute and let cool. Add that splash of vanilla mix in and then leave for moment. In another bowl mix the butter and sugar until smooth. Add the eggs and mix. Next, add the flour and mix all thoroughly together. Now take the date mixture you've been leaving aside and put it into the mixture of butter, castor sugar, flour and eggs. Mix well (the final mixture should be of pouring consistency). Bake for 25 minutes until springy to the touch.

Do not overcook as the pudding should be moist.

Toffee Sauce over page.

Mum's favourite summer fruit

TOFFEE SAUCE

YOU NEED

2 cups cream

2 cups soft brown sugar

METHOD

Put the cream and sugar in a saucepan and slowly bring to boil. Continue to gently simmer until sugar has melted and the sauce is a light brown colour. (If you want to make the sauce thinner just add more cream).

HOW TO SERVE

Cut healthy sized wedges of hot sticky toffee pudding and ladle with a pool of hot toffee sauce, allow this to run freely. Drizzle cream on the side. Add a handful of chopped strawberries and a mint leaf on top for decoration. If strawberries are out of season any berries will be just as delicious.

HINT: This recipe is great ammunition at any dinner

HOT RASPBERRY SOUFFLE

Serves 4

YOU NEED

2 tablespoons melted butter

4 egg whites

4 tablespoons castor sugar

6 tablespoons raspberries fresh or

tinned but drained

METHOD

Preheat oven to 350°f.

Grease four souffle dishes with a little melted butter. Place egg whites in mixing bowl and beat until frothy. Slowly add castor sugar and beat at the same time. When soft peaks appear stop beating and fold in raspberries. Spoon the mixture into souffle dishes and bake in hot oven of 350°f for ten minutes.

Wickedly indulging. Serve immediately.

CHAPTER TWELVE

CAKES AND AFTERNOON TEAS

Mum has a quick temper. She's allowed to being Irish. But her sense of humour always seems to outweigh her temper. I think she must have been going through a touch of the depressions. You'll see what I mean, when I relate the story.

Mum had just put one of her famous big chocolate cakes in the oven. About 20 minutes later the cake was almost ready and the chocolate aroma came wafting through from the kitchen. My Dad, brothers and I were discussing who would have the biggest piece and whether we'd have the will power not to eat the cake before the icing went on. Mum took the cake out of the oven, allowing it to cool in order to put our favourite fudge icing on.

The phone rang. It was for Mum. She was on the phone for what seemed an eternity. Imagine us, our tongues were hanging out for that delicious cake.

Temptation overcame us and we sneaked into the kitchen. We cut chunks out of that cake and it was so good but how to face Mum? We could blame the dog. While we were debating who would take the blame a hurricane in the form of Mum came storming at us. Who ate the chocolate cake? My dad said "I". Before he could get another word out in a state of total fury she grabbed the front of his shirt and buttons went flying in all directions. There was a deadly hush.

Dad cast his eyes down at the damage Mum had done and said meekly "Look what you've done Pet (he always called Mum Pet) that was my best shirt." Mum started crying and my brothers and I crept out of our hiding place. We all said sorry to Mum. Mind you, we did think at the time that she had over-reacted. It was only a chocolate cake after all. There was no need to rip Dad's shirt apart! Anyway, Mum saw the funny side of it, afterwards. Dad's shirt was beyond repair...his best shirt. So she bought him a new one.

The moral of the story...
its' a damn good chocolate cake.

afternoon tea in the garden

Apple Sour Cake

YOU NEED

$^1/_2$ cup butter

1 cup sugar

3 eggs

2 cups self raising flour

1 $^1/_2$ teaspoons cinnamon

2 teaspoons baking powder

1 cup apple puree or sauce

METHOD

Preheat oven to 350°f.
In a big bowl mix the butter until it's creamy white adding sugar gradually. Add eggs one at a time and mix well. Sift flour, cinnamon and baking powder together and gradually add to mixture.
Turn half of the mixture into greased baking tin, then spoon in the apple sauce and add remaining mixture.
Turn into greased cake tin. Bake in moderate oven 350°f for 35 minutes or until spongy to touch.

This apple sour cake is scrumptious with a very tart icing.

YOU NEED

1 cup icing sugar

$^1/_4$ cup lemon juice

METHOD

Simply mix together and drizzle over cake.

BIG CHOCOLATE CAKE

YOU NEED

1 $^1/_2$ cups self-raising flour

3 tablespoons cocoa

$^3/_4$ cups sunflower seed oil

1 cup castor sugar

1 cup boiling water

6 eggs separated

2 teaspoons baking powder

METHOD

Preheat oven to 400°f.

Sift flour and cocoa together into big mixing bowl and add sugar,oil and water. Mix well, add yolks of eggs. In a separate bowl place egg whites and beat until stiff. Now add beaten egg whites to above mixture, folding the egg white in lightly. Lastly fold in the baking powder. Turn into well-greased cake tin and bake at 400°f for 20 minutes or until springy to touch.

YOU NEED – ICING

2 tablespoons soft butter

1 large tablespoon cocoa

4 tablespoons drinking chocolate

2 cups icing sugar

dash vanilla

drizzle of water

METHOD

Just mix together and have fun icing.

Add crumbled chocolate (or use a flake chocolate) to top for decoration and extra taste treat.

UNCLE BILL'S DATE LOAF

YOU NEED
1 cup of boiling water
1 $^1/_2$ cups dates
1 teaspoon bi-carbonate soda
1 tablespoon butter
$^3/_4$ cup sugar
1 egg
1 $^1/_2$ cups flour
pinch of salt
1 $^1/_2$ teaspoons baking powder

METHOD
Preheat oven to 370°f.
Cut dates finely into a bowl and pour boiling water over
them. Then add bi-carbonate soda. Set aside until cool.
Put butter and sugar in a mixing bowl and beat until smooth.
Add egg and beat well, add date mixture and then flour and
salt. Lastly add baking powder and stir in well. Turn into
greased loaf tin and bake in moderate oven for half an hour.

P.S. Absolutely mouth watering served hot and buttery.

BANANA CAKE

YOU NEED

1/2 cup butter

1 cup sugar

2 eggs lightly beaten

2 cups bananas mashed

dash vanilla

pinch of salt

2 cups self-raising flour

1 teaspoon bi-carbonate soda

1/2 cup milk

METHOD

Preheat oven to 350°f.

In a big mixing bowl, mix the butter until it's very smooth and gradually add sugar, then eggs. Mix well, add mashed banana and vanilla. Sift salt, flour and bi-carbonate of soda together and add alternately with the milk. Turn into greased cake tin and bake in moderate oven 350°f for 20-25 minutes.

BANANA WALNUT CAKE

Add half a cup of walnuts or any nuts of your choice
to above mixture.

HINT: Instead of icing the banana cake try serving with
lashings of butter.

MISSISSIPPI MUD CAKE

A very rich, very thick, very chocolatey cake.

YOU NEED

1 1/2 cups butter chopped

1 cup dark chocolate grated

2 cups castor sugar

1 cup hot water

1/4 cup whisky

1 1/2 cups plain flour

1/4 cup self-raising flour

1/4 cup cocoa

3 eggs lightly beaten

METHOD

Preheat oven to 300°f.

Combine butter, chocolate, castor sugar, hot water and whisky in saucepan over low heat. Blend until chocolate has melted and mixture is smooth. Transfer chocolate mixture into mixing bowl. Sift together self-raising flour, plain flour,cocoa, add this to the chocolate mixture and then add the eggs, beat until smooth. Pour into medium sized greased cake tin and bake at 300°f for one hour or springy to touch.

DARK CHOCOLATE ICING
FOR MUD CAKE

YOU NEED

1 large slab dark chocolate (broken up)

3 teaspoons castor sugar

6 tablespoons cream

2 tablespoons cocoa

4 tablespoons drinking chocolate

4 tablespoons butter

splash Whisky (optional)

METHOD

Put the first five ingredients in a saucepan and gently heat until chocolate has melted – mix well. Remove from the stove and add the butter. Beat this in and add that splash of Whisky. Pour icing over the cooling cake and don't forget to lick the wooden spoon – it's wicked but sumptious.

CARROT CAKE

YOU NEED

1 cup self-raising flour
$^1/_2$ cup plain flour
$^1/_2$ cup sugar
$^1/_2$ teaspoon salt
1 teaspoon bi-carbonate soda
1 teaspoon cinnamon
$^1/_2$ cup tinned crushed pineapple
1 carrot grated
2 eggs
$^1/_2$ cup oil
dash vanilla
$^1/_2$ cup walnuts chopped

METHOD

Preheat oven to 300°f.
Sift the first six ingredients into a mixing bowl and add
pineapple, carrot, eggs, oil and vanilla. Beat until well
combined. Stir in walnuts, spoon mixture into a medium sized
greased tin and bake at 300°f for 20-25 minutes.
For frosting (icing) see next page.

LEMON FROSTING
FOR CARROT CAKE

YOU NEED

4 tablespoons soft butter

2 $1/2$ cups sifted icing sugar

3 tablespoons boiling water

$1/4$ cup lemon juice

METHOD

Place soft butter in mixing bowl. Slowly add sifted icing sugar mixing well. Just add a dash of boiling water at a time. The mixture should be like thickened cream. Now add the lemon juice. If you find the icing is too runny then add a little more sifted icing sugar and mix through.

This is a very simple and delicate icing for carrot cake.

The frosting, without the lemon, is a basic recipe and you can add flavour or colouring to suit your taste.

BAKED CHEESE CAKE

YOU NEED

2 cups sweet plain biscuits crumbed

$1/4$ cup melted butter

3 cups soft cream cheese

2 eggs

1 cup castor sugar

1 cup fresh cream

2 tablespoons custard powder

dash vanilla

METHOD – THE BASE

Combine biscuit crumbs and melted butter, press into a
22 cm pie dish and chill.

METHOD

Preheat oven at 300°f.
Put cream cheese, eggs, castor sugar, fresh cream and custard
powder into a big bowl. Beat like mad and add the vanilla.
The mixture should be creamy and smooth. Spoon into
crumb base and sprinkle a few biscuit crumbs on top. Bake at
300°f. When the cheese cake starts splitting on top it's done.
It should be pale gold on top. Use this as a basic cheese cake
recipe. You can add fruit but it is simply lovely made in
the traditional way.

Serve thick slices with good strong coffee.

AMERICAN-STYLE PANCAKES (PIKELETS)

Makes 10 -12 pikelets

The first time Mum made pancakes was hysterical. There we were, my brother and I waiting for the first pancake, maple syrup in hand, ready to pounce. Mum said stand back I'm going to flip it! The pancakes flew through the air and stuck to the ceiling. Mum tried a few more times but the same thing happened. By this time we were falling over each other laughing. Finally she made a batch of pancakes (no more flipping) and they were wonderful with lashings of maple syrup.

YOU NEED
3 cups self-raising flour
$1/2$ cup sugar
1 tablespoon oil
1 pinch salt
1 $1/2$ cups milk
2 eggs

METHOD
In a big bowl, place flour, sugar, oil, salt, half cup of the milk and the eggs. Mix well together to make a stiff dough . Now add the rest of the milk and mix until you have smooth thick batter. Brush a little oil over the pan and heat (medium-hot). The pancake mixture will pour easily if it's in a jug. Pour the batter into the centre of the pan and it will gently spread out. Watch for bubbles appearing on the surface of the pancake – time to flip it over. Cook other side until golden.

Serve the pancakes with maple syrup, cream and ice-cream. Also try maple syrup and lemon juice, orange and honey or butter, lemon and sugar.

HINT: Mum's rule, which never seems to fail, is to use plain flour for French crepes and self-raising for American pancakes and pikelets. Mum always adds oil to the mixture as this keeps the crepes, pancakes and pikelets nice and moist. Also makes it less likely that you'll have them sticking to the pan!!

whose turn to scrape the bowl?

CREPES

French crepes are a super stand by. Mum usually has a mixture made up. It's milk, flour and eggs so it will keep a few days in the refrigerator. When you make them, make sure they're really thin. This recipe is fine for crepe suzette, blintzes sweet or savoury, lemon crepes and many more.
Here are the recipes and some lovely fillings.

FRENCH CREPES

YOU NEED
1 cup plain flour
2 eggs
2 1/2 cups milk
1 tablespoon oil
pinch salt

METHOD
Mix all the ingredients together. If the mixture is too thick add more milk – the consistency should be like pouring cream. Make the crepes on a small pan (you can buy special crepe pans at most big stores) which has been rubbed over with oil. Pour a little mixture into the pan and tilt it so that the mixture spreads thinly covering the pan. The crepe will cook in seconds. When mottled gold on one side, flip over for a few seconds on to the other side. Stack them one on top of the other. This keeps them moist

CREPE SUZETTE

Or, as Mum really calls them 'crepes to stir the passions'.

YOU NEED – SAUCE
4 crepes (see page 186 for recipe)
4 tablespoons butter
3 tablespoons castor sugar
3 teaspoons finely grated orange rind
$1/2$ cup mixed liqueurs
(Grand Mariner, rum, brandy etc)

METHOD
Melt butter on small pan. Add castor sugar and orange rind.
Add liqueurs and simmer until hot and bubbly. Fold the
crepes in quarters and spoon the sauce over them and flame.

BLACK FOREST CREPE

Serves 4

YOU NEED

8 crepes (see recipe on page 186)
1 cup black cherries pitted (can use tinned)
$^1/_2$ cup thick cream
$^1/_2$ cup chocolate sauce (recipe to follow)

METHOD

Mix cherries and cream together. Place two tablespoons in
corner of crepe and roll. Pour chocolate sauce over crepe and
serve hot. Repeat above with remainder of crepes.

CHOCOLATE SAUCE

YOU NEED

1 cup dark chocolate buttons or pieces
1 cup cream
4 tablespoons drinking chocolate

METHOD

Melt chocolate over very low heat. Add cream and stir gently.
Now add drinking chocolate and stir into a rich creamy
consistency of dark, velvety, smooth chocolate – yum!

Muffins Texas With Bacon And Paprika

Makes 6

YOU NEED

2 eggs

1 cup milk

6 tablespoons melted butter

2 cups self-raising flour

2 teaspoons baking powder

$1/4$ teaspoon paprika

pinch salt and pepper

$1/2$ cup bacon cooked chopped finely

METHOD

Preheat oven to 400°f.
Beat eggs lightly, add milk and melted butter and beat lightly.
Then add flour, baking powder, paprika, salt and pepper.
Mix through gently, then add the bacon. Drop spoonfuls into
big, greased muffin pans just half filling them. Bake in hot
oven 400°f for 20 minutes until a pale golden colour.

P.S.   For basic muffin mixture simply omit the
bacon and paprika.

MUFFIN VARIATIONS

Here are several variations:

Cheese Muffins: *Add half a cup of grated cheese (cheddar or Swiss) to the basic muffin mixture on page 189.*

Smoked Salmon Muffins: *Add chopped smoked salmon and a little grated onion to the basic muffin mixture on page 189.*

Apple And Spice Muffins: *Add half grated apple, a teaspoon of mixed spice and four tablespoons of sugar to the original recipe on page 189.*

Blueberry Muffins: *Add one cup of blueberries which have just been rolled in flour and four tablespoons of sugar and add to the original recipe on page 189.*

Wholemeal Muffins: *Omit from original recipe one cup of self-raising flour and replace with one cup of wholemeal flour and half cup of sugar (see page 189 for the original recipe).*

SCONES

Makes 12

YOU NEED – BASIC RECIPE

2 $^1/_2$ cups self-raising flour

2 tablespoons sugar

2 teaspoons baking powder

4 tablespoons butter

$^1/_2$ cup milk

2 eggs well beaten

METHOD

Preheat oven to 350°f.
Mix dry ingredients together in bowl and add chopped butter
rubbing in the butter with fingertips until the mixture
resembles breadcrumbs. Add milk and well-beaten eggs.
Mix to a soft dough. Turn the mixture out onto a floured
board, pat the dough-like mixture out, keeping the dough
quite thick. Cut into with floured cutter – if you haven't got a
cutter then use the rim of a cup. Place the cut out dough on
baking tray, brush the top with cream or milk and sprinkle
with sugar. Bake in the pre-heated oven for 15 minutes.

An old fashioned classic. Serve hot with lots of butter,
strawberry jam and dollops of fresh clotted cream.
Don't forget the tea!

SCONES WITH SULTANAS

Just add a half cup of sultanas to the basic scone recipe.

PUMPKIN SCONES

YOU NEED

3 tablespoons sugar

6 tablespoons butter

1 egg

$1/2$ cup cream or milk

$3/4$ cup pumpkin (cooked and mashed)

2 $1/2$ cups self-raising flour

1 teaspoon baking powder

METHOD

Preheat oven to 230°f.
In a large bowl, mix the sugar and butter until smooth and add the egg and cream. Then add the cooked pumpkin. Now add the flour and baking powder combined. Roll dough out on floured board about 1 $1/2$cm thick and cut into rounds with floured cutter or rim of a cup. Brush a little cream on top and sprinkle a little sugar. Bake at 230°f for 20 minutes or until pale yellow and springy to touch.

Betty's Waffles

YOU NEED

1 cup plain flour

2 teaspoons baking powder

2 eggs beaten lightly

1 1/2 cups milk

1 cup cream

2 tablespoons oil

4 tablespoons melted butter

METHOD

Mix dry ingredients together, add beaten eggs, milk, cream,
oil and melted butter together. If batter is not thin enough
to pour then add a little more milk.

Heat waffle griddle really hot and pour batter into the griddle,
starting in the centre. Batter will spread out to fill the griddle.
Leave it closed until waffles have puffed and become golden
brown. Use a fork to lift waffle out.

Serve with lashings of maple syrup and family and friends will
adore you. Also great with ice-cream and at breakfast
with bacon and eggs.

CHAPTER THIRTEEN

PICNICS

I always feel like a child at the mention of a picnic.
I really don't mind where the picnic is. It could be on
the beach, beside a babbling brook, under a big old
gum tree in the bush, or maybe a picnic on a boat, in a
car, in a backyard or in a summer field... where the
jacaranda trees are all so heavy that their boughs
bend low. But just make sure you unpack platters of
wonderful food wherever it may be and let family
and friends feast.

my grandson Jack under the big old fig tree

SPICY CHICKEN WINGS

Serves 4

YOU NEED
1 kg chicken wings (or drumsticks,
whichever you prefer)
pinch of salt

MARINADE
$1/4$ cup honey
$1/4$ cup vinegar brown or white
$1/4$ cup soft brown sugar
$1/4$ cup soya sauce
1 clove garlic crushed

Combine all marinade ingredients together.

METHOD
Preheat oven to 350°f.
Cook chicken wings in boiling salted water for ten minutes.
Drain. Put chicken wings in roasting pan and pour over the
marinade – if possible, allow to marinate for an hour.
If not just pop in 350°f oven until wings are cooked through.

EASY PATE WITH PEPPERCORNS

YOU NEED

$^1/_2$ kg chicken livers

2 tablespoons butter

2 onions sliced finely

salt and pepper

$^1/_4$ cup sherry

1 tablespoon broken black pepper

$^1/_2$ teaspoon nutmeg

METHOD

Rinse the chicken livers in salty water. Plunge the chicken livers into a pot of fast boiling water for 30 seconds. Remove and strain. Melt butter in fry pan and cook the onions until soft. Add the chicken livers, salt and pepper. Then add sherry and peppercorns. Put all the mixture in a blender with the nutmeg and blend well.
Shape into mould which has been lined with glad wrap, then set down onto serving dish. Don't forget to remove glad wrap. Or you can put the mixture into individual serving pate dishes and decorate with slices of hard-boiled egg.
Serve cold.

BACON, EGG, SPINACH SALAD

Serves 6-8

YOU NEED – FOR SALAD
2 bunches English spinach
8 rashers bacon chopped without rind
6 eggs hardboiled and grated
(or chopped finely)

YOU NEED – FOR DRESSING
$1/4$ cup white vinegar
$1/4$ cup olive oil
1 teaspoon French mustard
1 tablespoon chives chopped
salt and pepper

METHOD
Fry bacon until crisp. Put aside on paper to drain fat off. Break
off stalks of spinach leaves and wash the leaves thoroughly but
gently, pat dry and keep refrigerated until needed.
Just before you leave for your picnic toss bacon and grated egg
with spinach leaves in a bowl with chives.

DRESSING
Mix vinegar, oil, mustard, chives, salt and pepper together.
Put in a bottle with tight lid and shake well. Take it with you
and add to spinach salad just before you serve.

SCOTCH EGGS

Serves 4

YOU NEED

4 eggs (hard boiled)
2 tablespoons plain flour
4 thick sausages
1 egg and $1/2$ cup milk blended together
1 cup of bread crumbs

METHOD

Hard boil four eggs then run them under cold water and shell.
Roll eggs lightly in flour. Take the skin off the sausages.
(Use one sausage for each egg). Fold or wrap sausage meat
evenly around the egg. Dip the scotch egg into the milk and
egg mixture, then roll in bread crumbs covering completely.
Now your Scotch eggs are ready to cook.

If you have a chip pan or deep pot put enough oil in one to
cover the eggs. The oil must be hot. Cook the eggs until
golden brown making sure the sausage meat is cooked
through. Drain the Scotch eggs on absorbent paper.
Cut length-wise and serve with a lovely salad.
Cooking time 15 minutes.

wildflower picnic

LOX BAGELS
(WITH SMOKED SALMON AND CREAM CHEESE)

YOU NEED

6 bagels

1 tub of cream cheese

6 slices of smoked salmon

1 onion sliced in rings thinly

1 tablespoon capers

1 teaspoon black pepper crushed

6 lemon wedges

METHOD

Cut the bagel through lengthwise, spread both sides
generously with cream cheese and add slices of smoked
salmon, onion ring, a few capers and a pinch of black pepper.
Sandwich together. Repeat with rest of bagels. You can add a
squeeze of lemon before eating. Bagels are more exciting than
sandwiches but if you prefer you can use sliced rye bread or
grainy brown instead of bagels.

SALMON MOUSSE

YOU NEED

1 teaspoon gelatine

$1/4$ cup white wine

$1/4$ cup lemon juice

2 cups tinned red salmon

1 large pickled gherkin grated

1 tablespoon Worcestershire sauce

$1/4$ cup cream

pinch of salt and pepper

dash of tabasco

1 teaspoon olive oil

(for greasing the fish mould)

3 eggs hard boiled

handful of cooked prawns

sprig of dill

METHOD

Keep hard-boiled eggs for later. Soak gelatine in the wine and
dissolve over a pot of hot water. Add lemon juice.
Flake (separate) salmon, add gherkin and all other ingredients.
Mix with the gelatine. Grease a fish mould with oil. Slice the
hard-boiled eggs and place slices along the centre of mould.
Fill mould with salmon mix and chill until set.
When ready to serve turn out on serving dish and decorate
with prawns and dill.

SANDWICH STACK

Serves 4

YOU NEED
8 slices of wholegrain bread (crusts removed)
8 slices pastrami
2 tablespoons hot chutney
2 shallots finely cut

METHOD
Pile pastrami and chutney onto bread, sprinkle with shallots
and sandwich together.

NICOISE BAGUETTE

Serves 6

YOU NEED

2 large baguettes (French loaves)
$^1/_2$ block butter
1 mignotte lettuce
(ask your green grocer or just use a lettuce
you're familiar with – makes no difference,
except minute looks great)
$^1/_2$ cup tinned tuna drained and
flaked (separated)
12 black olives pitted
(pips taken out) and chopped
3 boiled eggs shelled and sliced
$^1/_2$ cup French dressing (see recipe page 101)

METHOD

Prepare loaves by chopping each baguette into three sections
then slice halfway through each section and butter. Add
lettuce, two tablespoons of tuna, a few chopped olives and
three to four slices of egg. Repeat with rest of loaf sections.
Take French dressing along in picnic basket and add a drizzle
to baguettes before serving.

SALAMI BAGUETTE

Serves 4

YOU NEED

2 baguettes (French loaves)
$^1/_4$ block butter
1 lettuce (of your choice)
$^1/_2$ salami sliced thinly
2 tomatoes sliced thinly
6 slices Swiss cheese

METHOD

Cut loaves into three sections and slit each section halfway through. Don't go all the way through – all that filling will fall out. Butter lightly and pile full of all the Continental ingredients.

HINT: You can buy traditional small baguettes but if you can't find any the long baguettes are great.

HINT: Fill the spaces in your picnic basket with lots of exotic fruits and when you serve squeeze lemon juice over cut fruit. It brings out all the flavours.

POPPY SEED CAKE

Serves 8

YOU NEED

3/4 cup hot milk

3/4 cup poppy seeds

6 tablespoons butter

1 1/2 cups sugar

3 cups self-raising flour

1 teaspoon baking powder

1 cup cold milk

4 egg whites beaten until stiff

METHOD

Preheat oven to 370°f.

Pour hot milk over poppy seeds and allow to soak for two
hours. Cream butter and sugar together until fluffy. Now add
the poppy seed mixture and mix well together. Add flour and
baking powder then the cold milk. Gently add the stiff egg
whites. Pour mixture into a 22cm baking dish.

Bake in 370°f oven for 25 minutes.

This is a surprise picnic basket treat.

HINT: Don't forget – champagne, glasses, picnic rug and
thermos of coffee, napkins (lots), salt and pepper.

Have fun!

CHAPTER FOURTEEN

CHRISTMAS LUNCH

You may wonder what this next story has to do with Christmas fare! Just read on and you'll see. Mum was returning from a short holiday in Ireland, rushing back to be with us for Christmas. We really had missed her. Dad isn't the best cook (except for his barbecues) and my brothers and I were looking a bit thin, plus Mum had a suitcase-full of our Gran's Christmas presents.

To cut a long story short, the first stop on her journey home was Zurich where the plane was to re-fuel and take on more passengers.
I'll let Mum take over from here:

"There was a delay because of a bomb scare. All the passengers were rushed off the plane into a waiting room where various officials were pacing up and down staring at us with beady eyes of suspicion.
Finally, two security officers entered the room and hollered out my name. I nearly died! Eventually I raised my trembling hand and said: "That's me".
"Come with us," they ordered.

All the other passengers were staring at me and I knew that I certainly wouldn't get any help from that lot.

By this time I was in a state, thinking that I'd never see
my children or my dear husband again. I was ushered
into a windowless room with a bright spotlight and
there centred on a table was my suitcase. One of the
men started cutting open its top with a rather evil-
looking knife. I thought that this couldn't be
happening and piped up: "What do you think you're
doing?" They unpacked everything one by one.

Finally, they seemed to come across what they were
looking for. I had bought my son a toy telephone – red
metal, large handle, lots of buttons, knobs and a million
wires entangled around Gran's Christmas pudding
(I suppose under X-ray it did look rather suspicious).
I picked up the red metal box, untangled the Christmas
pudding and pressed a few buttons (I'm sure all the
security men stepped back because they expected an
explosion), as I did this a little voice from within the
phone repeated over and over: "Is your Mummy home.
Is your Mummy home?"

Everyone burst out laughing (much to my relief)
realising I wasn't some mad terrorist. The only thing
lethal in my bag was Gran's famous Christmas pudding,
lethal for all the brandy she pours into it!" So with the
all-clear to take off, Mum made it safely home.
We gobbled down that Christmas pudding and after all
these years we've lost track of that toy telephone
but not Gran's recipe.

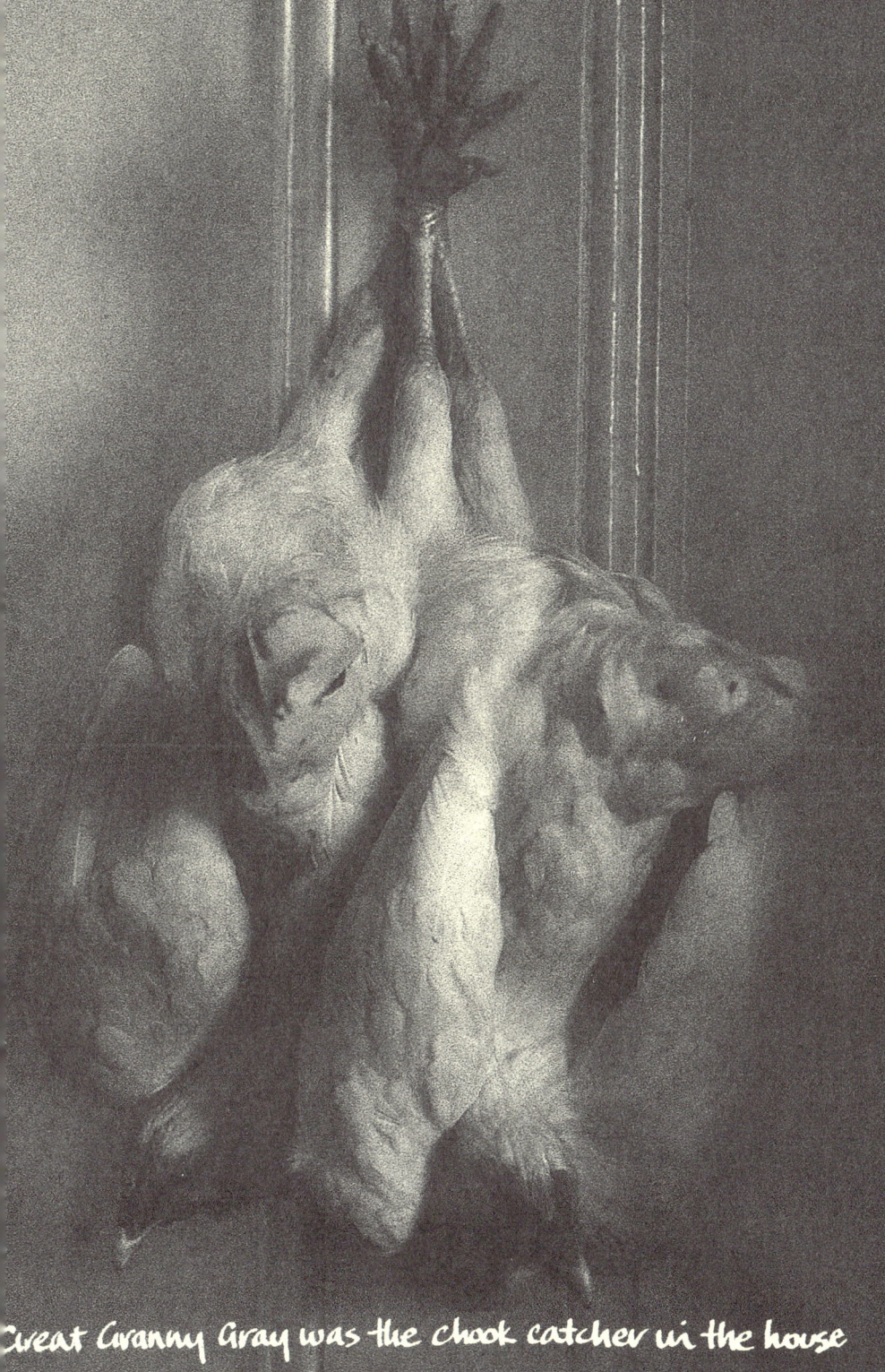

Great Granny Gray was the chook catcher in the house

ROAST TURKEY WITH CHRISTMAS STUFFING

Serves 10

YOU NEED

7kg turkey

3 cups sage and onion stuffing

$1/2$ cup boiling water

1kg sausage meat

1 tablespoon flour

1 tablespoon powdered ginger

1 tablespoon salt

1 cup brandy

$1/2$ cup orange juice

METHOD – FOR STUFFING

Preheat oven at 300°f.

Mix sage and onion with half cup of boiling water.
Add sausage meat and mix thoroughly. Our gran adds grated
carrot and celery to her stuffing mix. You might like to try it.

METHOD – ROASTING TURKEY

Place the turkey on a roasting pan and stuff with the prepared
stuffing. Rub entire surface of bird with flour, ginger and salt
combined. Mix the brandy the orange juice together and pour
this delicious nectar over the turkey.
Cover with foil and cook for one and a half hours.
Frequently spoon the sediment juice from the roast over the
turkey. If it's a tough old turkey, cook for another hour.

The following recipes starting over the page are the best
accompaniments for your turkey Christmas dinner.

HINT: Use left over jams mixed with a bit of brandy – it's a
quick and wonderful glaze for turkey.

TURKEY GRAVY

QUICK STEPS METHOD

Remove turkey from roasting pan. Pour off excess fat. Then add three tablespoons of flour to sediment left in pan. Stir and cook until dark brown. Add two cups of water and stir well until combined. Add a good splash of sherry and stir in. If the gravy is too thick add more water. When the right consistency strain and keep hot in gravy boat.

CRANBERRY JELLY

Serves 8

YOU NEED
4 cups cranberries
2 cups sugar
2 cups water

METHOD
Wash cranberries then toss into saucepan and mix roughly with a wooden spoon. Add water, and stew until soft. Rub through a seive, add the sugar and re-heat for two minutes. Pour into glass jar and chill.

P.S. Of course, if you're in a mad rush you can buy it at the supermarket.

the family heirlooms

ROAST POTATOES

YOU NEED
15 small potatoes peeled
$^{1}/_{2}$ teaspoon salt
$^{1}/_{2}$ teaspoon pepper

METHOD
Sprinkle salt and pepper over potatoes. Add potatoes to turkey
roast about 45 minutes before turkey is done.
Turning occasionally.
They can also be roasted in deep fat if you prefer.

ALTERNATIVE METHOD
Peel potatoes and boil in salted water for about ten minutes.
Roll in flour. Heat oil in pot enough to cover the potatoes.
When the oil is very hot add the potatoes and cook until
golden and crisp.

HONEYED CARROTS

YOU NEED
6 medium carrots chopped lengthways
$^{1}/_{4}$ cup butter
$^{1}/_{4}$ cup honey
a pinch of salt

METHOD
Bring water to boil in saucepan. Add carrots and cook until
tender for 10-15 minutes. Drain water off. Then toss in honey
and butter. Add a sprinkle of salt. Simple and sweet.

BRUSSEL SPROUTS

YOU NEED

30 brussel sprouts

2 tablespoons melted butter

pinch of salt

METHOD

Remove wilted leaves, cut off stems of brussel sprouts.
Bring water to boil Add prepared brussel sprouts and salt.
Cover and cook until tender for 10-20 minutes.
When ready toss the sprouts in butter.

CHRISTMAS FRUIT PIES

Makes 24

YOU NEED – FOR FILLING

4 tablespoons butter

4 cups mixed dried fruit

1/2 cup soft brown sugar

1/2 cup lemon juice

1 teaspoon mixed spice

1/2 teaspoon powdered nutmeg

1/2 teaspoon cinnamon

1/4 cup brandy

1/4 cup whisky

3 apples chopped very finely

1 airtight jar

METHOD

Mix all the ingredients together and spoon into jars with airtight lids. It's best kept this way for a week as it plumps up the fruit. However, if you haven't the time, you can buy some really great fruit mince mixture on the shelves in any supermarket. Now read on... my gran's famous Christmas fruit pies are about to hit the world.

See over page for pastry recipe.

YOU NEED – PASTRY
6 sheets of puff pastry
2 tablespoons melted butter
$1/4$ cup milk
2 patty tins giving you 24 fruit pies
$1/2$ cup icing sugar

METHOD
Preheat oven at 450°f.
Place a sheet of puff pastry on floured board. Cut the bottom
rounds slightly larger than the top rounds to fit patty tins.
For example, 24 large pastry rounds and 24 smaller ones (a
glass is pretty good for cutting the rounds).
Grease the patty tins with the melted butter and place 24 large
rounds in each section. Put large spoonfuls of the fruit mixture
in each patty section. Cover with smaller rounds of pastry and
press the edges of the pastry together.
Brush a little milk over the top and bake in 450°f for 25
minutes or until golden brown. Allow to cool and then
sprinkle with icing sugar.

Mum always make dozens of Christmas pies.
Honestly, there are never enough! Usually, on Christmas Eve
Mum has to make an extra batch for Christmas Day as we
gobble the lot the night before.

CHRISTMAS CAKE

YOU NEED

2 cups mixed dried fruit

1 $^1/_2$ cups plain flour

2 teaspoons baking powder

1 teaspoon mixed spice

1 teaspoon cinnamon

pinch of salt

$^1/_2$ cup of almonds chopped

$^1/_2$ cup glace cherries

6 eggs

$^1/_2$ cup brandy or whisky

$^3/_4$ cup butter

1 cup soft brown sugar

2 tablespoons golden syrup

METHOD

Pre-heat oven to 350°f.

Wash the dried fruit, dry thoroughly (this is so the flour
adheres properly to the fruit). Sieve the flour, baking powder,
mixed spice, cinnamon and salt together.

Add the dried fruit, chopped almonds and cherries, mix.
Beat the eggs and brandy together in separate bowl. Beat the
butter, sugar and golden syrup in another bowl.

Phew... next step!! Add half the flour and half of the egg
mixture to the butter mixture. Mix this thoroughly with a
wooden spoon. Once that's done add the remainder of the
flour and the egg mixture. Once again mix thoroughly.
This has to be mixed well to keep air through the mixture. If
you plonk it all in, you cake will be far too stodgy and heavy.
Line a 23cm cake tin or something near to that with double
grease-proof paper, base and sides.
Bake for two and a half hours at 350°f and then for a further
one and a half hours at 270°f.

MILLE FEUILLES

Serves 10

YOU NEED

4 puff pastry sheets

METHOD

Preheat oven 470°f.
Place the pastry on a lightly floured board. Cut the two sheets
in half and bake on a greased baking tray for ten minutes.
Don't let the pastry sheets overlap. Then lower oven heat to
350°f and bake the pastry until a pale golden brown.
Remove from oven, set aside to cool.

Now for the luscious home-made custard filling.

YOU NEED

1 tablespoon butter
3 tablespoons flour
2 cups milk
3 tablespoon castor sugar
2 egg yolks (lightly beaten)
splash of vanilla essence
splash of Bailey's Irish Cream
$1/2$ cup raspberry jam
icing sugar

See next page for method.

METHOD

Melt the butter in saucepan. Add the flour mix quickly and then cook for a couple of minutes.

Gradually, add the milk, stir over a low heat until the mixture comes to boiling point. Gently cook for two minutes.

Add sugar and remove the saucepan from the heat. When cool, add the lightly beaten yolk of eggs, vanilla essence and Bailey's Irish Cream. Mix well and put saucepan back on gentle heat. Cook until the custard thickens.

Don't reboil. Let stand and cool.

ASSEMBLING THE LAYERS

Sandwich two layers of pastry together with raspberry jam and custard. Repeat this with another two layers of pastry, jam and custard. Sprinkle the top with icing sugar. When serving use a sharp knife to cut gently through the layers.

This is the family's favourite Christmas dessert
– cool and light.
Happy Christmas!

GREAT GRANDMOTHER GRAY'S CHRISTMAS PUDDING

YOU NEED

1 $^{1}/_{2}$ cups butter (soft)

1 cup stale bread crumbs (you can buy packet
bread crumbs)

2 cups sugar

$^{1}/_{4}$ cup ground almonds

1 tablespoon mixed spice

$^{1}/_{2}$ teaspoon nutmeg

1 cup self-raising flour

6 eggs beaten

2 cups seedless raisons

2 cups sultanas

2 cups currants

1 cup chopped glace cherries

1 cup brandy (if you only have whisky in the
cupboard that's okay)

$^{1}/_{4}$ cup orange juice

P.S. You'll also need a pudding cloth (tea towel, calico or
pretty Christmas cloth)and string for tying it up.

METHOD

Mix the soft butter and breadcrumbs together in a large bowl.
When thoroughly mixed together add the sugar, almonds,
mixed spice, nutmeg and half the flour. Mix well. Now, add
the beaten eggs. In a separate bowl place the dried fruit and
the cherries with the remaining flour. Mix together and then
add the main mixture. Now the part Great Gran is famous for
– the brandy and orange juice, add this with a steady hand
and stir well with a wooden spoon. Yes, it must be a wooden

spoon as it makes the mixture lighter. Pour the mixture into the pudding cloth and tie securely with string. Place in a bowl and steam for five hours in a large pot of water. Don't let the water cover the top of the pudding.

HINT: Try to make the pudding a couple of weeks before Christmas. And then – a few days before Christmas throw a half cup of brandy over it.

P.S. I know it seems like a long-drawn out recipe but honestly it's worth it. Serve with Brandy Sauce.

BRANDY SAUCE

YOU NEED
2 egg yolks
$^1/4$ cup castor sugar
2 egg whites
$^1/4$ cup fresh cream
$^1/4$ cup brandy

METHOD
Beat the egg yolks and castor sugar together in a saucepan over a pot of boiling water until thick and smooth. Remove from heat. Add stiffly beaten egg whites and heat again (don't boil). Next, add the brandy and cream. Now, you're ready to serve with your Christmas pudding.

P.S. Oh! Don't forget to wrap coins in tinfoil and push into the pudding as the children will definitely have second helpings to look for the money.
And yes, it would be easier to buy a pudding but believe you me it'll never taste like my Great Grandmother Gray's.

CHAPTER FIFTEEN

DAD'S BARBECUE

It wouldn't seem right if my Dad's barbecues were not included in Mum's cook book. Over the years, Dad has cooked the most outstanding barbecues.

When we were younger we lived on the edge of the bush, our garden was almost an extension of the bush.

Dad built a wonderful barbecue in the garden. We spent many a happy evening around the fire with the tall gum trees encircling us. At the first whiff of meat cooking the kookaburras would become quite excited and let us know very loudly they expected a morsel or two as they swooped down beside the fire.

Isn't it strange how it sometimes decides to rain when you're half way through cooking the meat.

Murphy's law! Well, that didn't deter Dad. The garden umbrellas were swiftly set up over the fire, it was quite a funny sight – Dad standing there totally oblivious to the rain belting down.

We loved the rainy barbecues because, after we had devoured the succulent food we sat snuggled around the blazing fire under the umbrellas telling ghost stories. Mum always had the scariest ones, she used to terrify all our friends. Then we'd have a singing competition, with the kookaburras joining in and the ghosts taking flight.

Dad's barbecue chicken legs

The fine evenings were many too. We'd gather in the
garden for a barbecue at sunset with a radiant sky all
round. Looking back, I think the garden was a 'magic'
garden, it was so peaceful and we miss being there. Dad
still makes great barbecues but there's something
missing. I wish we lived in that house again with the
magic garden on the edge of the bush. I could go on
and on about the barbecue evenings but I'd better get
Dad's recipes down on paper and you can make your
own magical evenings or days.

DAD'S HINTS FOR SUCCESSFUL BARBECUES

✦ *Dad never uses gas barbecues.*
He says you may as well fry the meat in a pan!
Wood fires are best. They give flavour to the meat.

✦ *First thing he does to prepare this famous event is to scrunch*
up lots of newspaper. Then he places it in the barbecue with lots
of thin, dry wood on top and sets it alight.
The wood will catch alight quickly. When the fire really gets
going throw more dry wood on.

✦ *Don't start cooking the meat until the flames have subsided*
and the fire has a base of hot embers.
This way, the meat doesn't overcook and become dry.

✦ *You can buy different types of kindling for barbecues.*
You can also collect pine cones if you have a pine tree near
— you'll need lots.

✦ *It's a good idea to buy meat in advance as it gives you lots of*
time to marinade.

✦ *Never sprinkle salt over the meat before cooking.*
It extracts all the juices and dries meat out.

✦ *Whilst barbecuing meat, resist the temptation to turn it*
constantly. It really makes it tough.

✦ *Don't forget to oil the grid or tray on top of the fire. This prevents the meat sticking.*

✦ *Start with the thickest pieces of meat. They take the longest cooking time.*

✦ *If you are having a large barbecue party, chicken is a great standby. The most important point to remember with chicken is to cook it over a very low fire for a longer time than meat.*

✦ *When you've done all the cooking throw lots of wood on the fire, really get it going, ready for all your ghost stories.*

STEAKS

The following steaks are suitable for barbecuing:
T-bones (trim off fat)
Fillet of beef sliced
Scotch fillet sliced
Rib steak sliced

YOU NEED – FOR MARINADE
$1/4$ cup tomato sauce
$1/4$ cup any vinegar
2 tablespoons Worcestershire sauce
1 clove garlic crushed
1 cup red wine
1 onion finely chopped
1 teaspoon paprika
1 teaspoon cayenne pepper
1 teaspoon black pepper crushed

METHOD
Mix all ingredients together in a deep dish. Marinate meat for
two hours. When the meat is on the barbecue, spoon the
remainder of the marinade over it frequently. And don't
forget – resist turning the meat constantly, it's a no no!

LOIN OF LAMB CHOPS
WITH HERB MARINADE

Serves 6

YOU NEED

12 chops

$1/2$ cup white vinegar

$1/2$ cup beer

2 cloves garlic crushed (optional)

$1/2$ cup fresh mint chopped

1 teaspoon rosemary

pinch salt and pepper

METHOD

Trim the chops and leave aside. Then mix above ingredients together. Pour over chops and allow to stand for a couple of hours or as long as possible. Remove chops from marinade and pop onto barbecue. Spoon the marinade over the chops frequently while cooking.

TOMATO AND ONION SAUCE

This is a lovely rich sauce to serve with any barbecued meat.

YOU NEED

1 tablespoon butter

2 onions chopped finely

2 cups tinned peeled tomatoes, retain liquid

1/4 cup tomato sauce

1/4 cup Worcestershire sauce

dash tabasco sauce

1 tablespoon any mustard

1 tablespoon tomato paste

1 tablespoon brown sugar

METHOD

Melt butter in fry pan, add onions and cook until soft.
Add the tomatoes and liquid. Mix and cook for ten minutes.
Toss in rest of ingredients and cook gently for 20 minutes.

BARBECUE CHICKEN

Serves 4

YOU NEED

6 chicken breasts

$1/4$ cup lemon juice

2 tablespoons olive oil

1 teaspoon salt

1 teaspoon pepper

METHOD

Leave chicken breasts aside. Mix all the other ingredients
together to create a simple marinade for keeping the chicken
moist. Brush this marinade over the entire surface of the
chicken breasts. Now, place on barbecue – keep the fire very
low. Turn the chicken frequently (unlike meat you may turn
the chicken as often as you wish).
Spoon remainder of the marinade over the chicken.
You can tell the chicken is ready when the flesh is white and
it's beautifully crispy on the outside.

KEBABS AND HONEY SAUCE

Serves 6

YOU NEED
2 kg lamb cubed
2 onions chopped in wedges
6 rashers bacon without rind
1 green capsicum seeded and chopped
15 wooden skewers

YOU NEED – FOR MARINADE
$1/4$ cup olive oil
3 tablespoons soya sauce
2 tablespoons Worcestershire sauce
$1/4$ cup fresh lemon juice
$1/4$ cup honey
1 clove garlic crushed (optional)

METHOD
Combine all marinade ingredients together. Mix well and it's
ready. Next get your kebabs going by arranging lamb pieces,
onion, bacon and capsicum on skewer. Repeat this using up
all the skewers. Place in dish and pour marinade over kebabs.
Allow to marinate for at least two hours, longer if possible.
Barbecue for six minutes either side by spooning the marinade
over the kebabs frequently.

PEPPER SAUCE FOR CHICKEN

YOU NEED

3 tablespoons butter

1 clove garlic crushed

2 onions grated finely

1 red capsicum seeded and chopped

1 green capsicum seeded and chopped

2 tablespoons flour

2 teaspoons cayenne

pinch of salt and pepper

$1/4$ cup tomato puree

$1/4$ cup white wine (optional)

1 tablespoon sweet chutney

METHOD

Melt butter in fry pan. Add garlic, onion and capsicums.
Cook until soft and then add flour, cayenne, salt and pepper.
Mix well, add tomato puree, sweet chutney and wine.
Cook gently until thickened.

This is my favourite sauce.

SAUSAGES

There's no hard and fast rule on sausages. There are so many different varieties to choose from so go for what you like. These are some of the many varieties: tomato and onion, garlic, chicken, herb, country beef, satay, spicy, lamb, Italian pork, hot Italian, Mercuez (very hot) Mexican, Malaysian, chicken with sesame and chicken with black pepper.

METHOD

Prick all over with a fork and just toss on the barbecue for about 15 minutes.

BARBECUED PRAWNS

Serves 6

YOU NEED

30 large green prawns
$^{1}/_{2}$ cup fresh lemon juice
$^{1}/_{2}$ cup butter melted
2 tablespoons soya sauce

METHOD

Slit prawns along back, remove veins and leave head and shell
on. They retain much more flavour that way. Marinate in
soya sauce for five minutes turning them frequently.
Remove prawns from soya sauce. Mix the lemon juice and
butter together and dip each prawn in to this mixture.
Then throw on the barbie!!
Cook very gently for five minutes, turn over and cook
another few minutes until a lovely pink colour.

POTATO SALAD

Serves 8

YOU NEED

8 potatoes cooked in jackets (keeps their
flavour better)
2 hard-boiled eggs sliced
1 onion chopped finely
pinch of salt
1 teaspoon paprika
$1/4$ cup French dressing
$1/4$ cup mayonnaise
2 tablespoons chives

METHOD

Peel and cube potatoes into bowl. Add eggs, onion and
seasoning. Pour over the French dressing and allow to
marinate for a couple of hours if possible.
Before serving, add the mayonnaise and mix gently.
Sprinkle with chives.

CAESAR SALAD

Serves 4

YOU NEED

1 Cos lettuce (ask your green grocer if you're
not sure what a Cos lettuce looks like)

1/2 bunch curly endive

1 clove garlic crushed

2 tablespoons olive oil

1 cup croutons

1 tablespoon flat anchovy chopped

1 egg beaten

1/4 cup freshly grated parmesan cheese

1/4 cup lemon juice

1 tablespoon Worcestershire sauce

pinch of salt and black pepper

METHOD

Break lettuce and endive into salad bowl. Combine garlic and
oil together and drizzle over lettuce and endive. Add croutons
and anchovies. Combine egg, parmesan cheese, lemon juice,
Worcestershire sauce and seasoning – beat well.
Pour over salad just before serving and grate a little extra
parmesan cheese over the top.

P.S. For recipe on croutons see page 52

CHAPTER SIXTEEN

MIDNIGHT SNACKS
& HOT TODDIES

It was a funny and strange story, and one I remember as if it happened yesterday. Mum awakened with a start, she had been in a deep sleep when she opened her eyes, blinked a few times and focused. She looked out of the window, straining her eyes, as if compelled. "It can't be," she thought! "I'm seeing things".

The saucer shaped object, with little round windows, moved closer. She became really excited, fear didn't enter her head as she dashed to our bedrooms begging us to "come quickly, put your clothes on, something warm, there's a flying saucer outside!" We tripped over each other to get dressed and out of the front door. This isn't the first flying saucer Mum's seen by the way.

We stood in the garden waiting for the flying saucer! Mum is still convinced to this day that there was one up there. Maybe, had we not gone outside with her...who knows what would have happened? But she wanted to share whatever it was with us. I told her that 'we could have been space orphans' if they had landed and whisked her away to the unknown! For nights after, she searched the sky. "Perhaps third time lucky," she said. Mum never lived that evening down.

So if your Mum happens to get you up in the middle of the night to watch weird space things, the least she can do for you is make some midnight snacks.

We had a great feast that night and Mum had a hot toddy. In fact, she'd probably had a few before spotting that flying saucer!

Isn't this what midnight snacks are all about?

Bacon, Lettuce And Tomato Stack (B.L.T.)

Serves 2

YOU NEED

4 slices of bread

4 tablespoons butter

6 rashers of cooked chopped bacon

4 lettuce leaves

2 tomatoes

4 tablespoons mayonnaise

METHOD

Toast bread and then butter while it's still hot.

On first slice of toasted bread place several pieces of bacon.

Top this with second piece of toast and add lettuce leaves.

Top with third slice and add tomato and mayonnaise.

Finally, the forth piece of toast and ready to bite.

HINT: Could be a good idea to hold sandwich
together with a skewer.

IRISH RAREBIT

Serves 4

YOU NEED

4 slices of buttered toast

1 tablespoon butter

$1/2$ cup milk

1 tablespoon flour

1 teaspoon paprika

1 teaspoon French mustard

$1/2$ cup beer

1 cup grated cheddar cheese

METHOD

Melt the butter in a saucepan, mix in the flour and stir,
gradually pouring in the milk bring to boil.
Cook gently and it should be creamy and thick in texture.
Add the seasoning and mustard. And don't forget the beer!
Toss in the cheese and allow to melt. Pour this mixture onto
hot buttered toast. Sprinkle with paprika and pop under the
grill until golden and bubbling.

FRESH FRUIT SMOOTHIE

Serves 2

YOU NEED
1 cup mixed fruit chopped
(strawberries, bananas, melon... use whatever
your heart desires.)
2 cups milk
4 tablespoons ice-cream
(you can use yoghurt if you prefer)

METHOD
Toss all ingredients into blender and whizz together for one
minute. Pour into a tall glass and enjoy.
Wonderful on hot nights when you can't sleep.

BANANA AND PINEAPPLE GRILL

YOU NEED

4 slices thick bread

2 tablespoons butter

4 slices leg ham

2 bananas

$^1/_2$ tin pineapple pieces drained

4 slices cheese of your choice

METHOD

Preheat the grill and toast the bread. Butter it and place ham on each slice of bread. Then add slices of banana and a few pieces of pineapple. Top with cheese and pop under the grill until golden brown. Enjoy, it's a wonderful snack.

GIANT RYE SANDWICH

Serves 2

YOU NEED

2 slices of rye bread

6 slices of Camembert cheese

1 ripe avocado

1 tomato sliced

lots of lettuce

splash of French dressing (page 101)

METHOD

Butter rye bread and pile it all on – scrumptious!

Egg Nog

YOU NEED

4 mugs milk

4 eggs

4 tablespoons sugar

4 tablespoons brandy (optional)

METHOD

Pour milk into saucepan and bring to boil.

Whisk in the eggs and remove from the heat.

Add the sugar and for heaven's sake don't forget the brandy.

Hot Chocolate
With Flakey Bars

For teetotallers

YOU NEED
4 cups hot milk
6 tablespoons drinking chocolate
2 Cadbury flakes
4 mugs

METHOD
Pour milk into saucepan and bring to boil.
Then whisk in the drinking chocolate. Pour into mugs and
sprinkle each one with a Cadbury flake, or if you hate that
add a couple of marshmallows to the hot chocolate.
They melt and become quite luscious.

Have a cup of tea if you want to be really boring.

IRISH COFFEE

YOU NEED

4 strong glasses or Irish coffee mugs

1 bottle Irish Whiskey

(only joking 4 tots of Irish Whiskey will do)

1 big pot strong coffee

4 tablespoons sugar

(maybe more if you have a sweet tooth)

1 cup cream

METHOD

Pour a tot of whiskey into each glass. Top up with coffee and sugar (to taste). Then, very slowly pour some cream over the back of a dessert spoon into the coffee. If you pour really carefully the cream should form a layer on the top. If that's too difficult, just put a blob of (whipped) cream on the top of the coffee. It will taste great anyway. And "the top of the mornin' to you too!!"

Hot Punch

YOU NEED

1 bottle red wine

1 cup castor sugar

1 stick cinnamon

$1/4$ teaspoon cloves powdered

$1/4$ cup lemon juice fresh

$1/4$ lemon rind

METHOD

Pop all the ingredients into a pot and bring to boiling point.
Serve in strong glasses.

If you put a silver spoon in the glass it won't crack. Well, it
seems to work for Mum.
So good luck!

CHAPTER SEVENTEEN

OVEN TEMPERATURES

You might not want to delve into this chapter but if
you don't your cakes could be:

too dry

too high

too heavy

too small

too sticky

too hard

or

nothing at all

Important note: all recipes in My Mum's Cook Book are
cooked in an electric Fahrenheit oven.
Check the chart below for conversions:

ELECTRIC TEMPERATURES

	Fahrenheit	**Celsius**
Very Slow	250°	120°
Slow	300°	150°
Moderately slow	325°–350°	160°–180°
Moderate	375°–400°	190°–200°
Moderately hot	425°–450°	220°–230°
Hot	475°–500°	250°–260°
Very hot	525°–550°	270°–290°

See over page for Gas temperatures.

what's cooking?

GAS TEMPERATURES

	Fahrenheit	Celsius
Very slow	250°	120°
Slow	277°-300°	140°-150°
Moderately slow	325°	160°
Moderate	350°	180°
Moderately hot	375°	190°
Hot	400°-450°	200°-230°
Very hot	475°-500°	250°-260°

YOUR OWN COOK BOOK

INDEX